I0823017
CURSED PRINCESS CLUB
LambCat

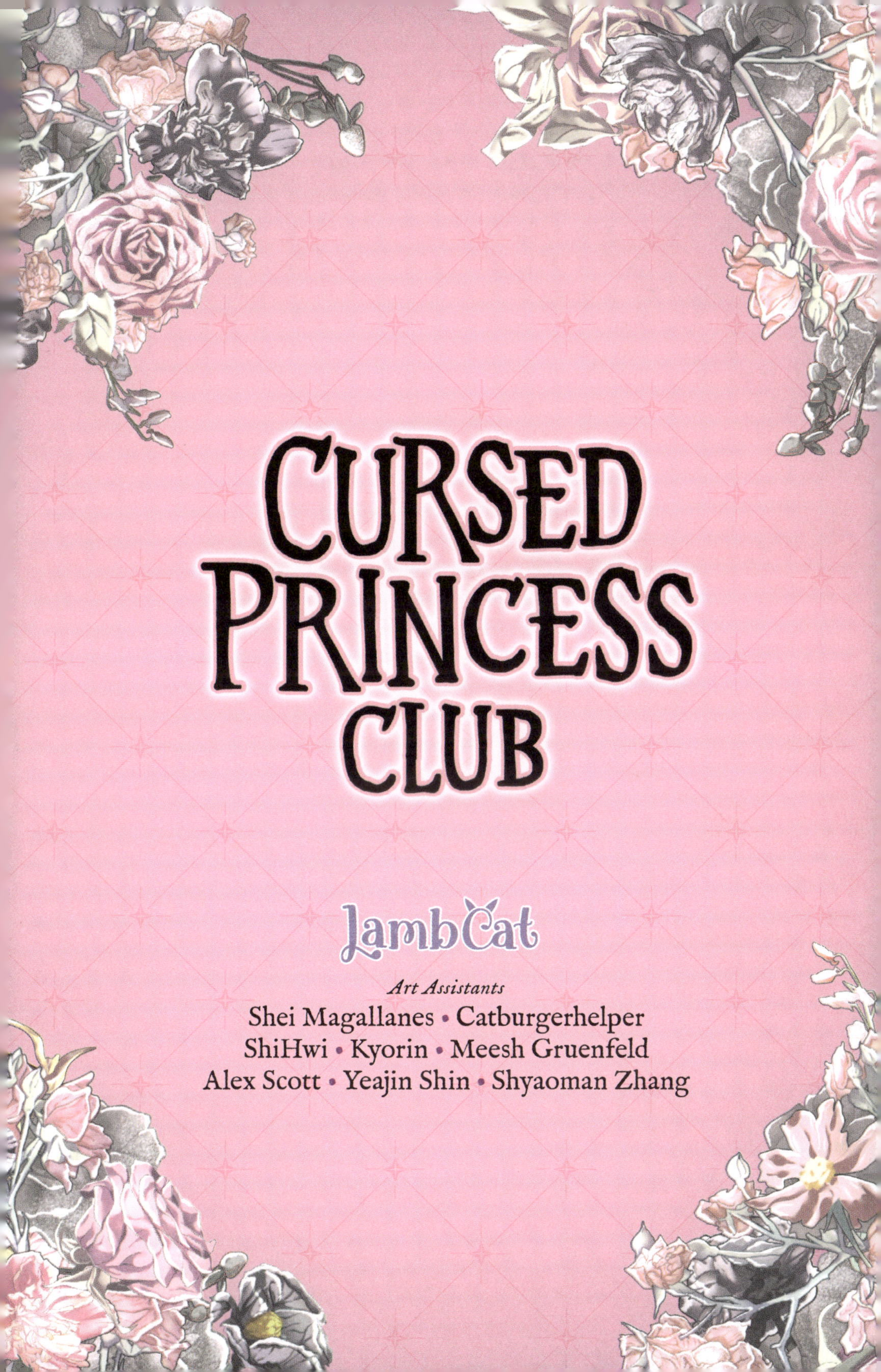

CURSED PRINCESS CLUB

LambCat

Art Assistants

Shei Magallanes • Catburgerhelper
ShiHwi • Kyorin • Meesh Gruenfeld
Alex Scott • Yeajin Shin • Shyaoman Zhang

EMMA HAMBLY *Editor*
JOSH BEATMAN *Cover Design*
NIKO DALCIN *Publication Design*
NIKO DALCIN *Sequential Story Design*
PATRICK McCORMICK *Senior Manager, Production*
DELANEY ANDERSON *Production Editor*
EUNICE BAIK *Original WEBTOON Editor*

Cursed Princess Club Volume 4

Copyright © 2025, Wattpad WEBTOON Studios, Inc. All rights reserved.
Published in Canada by WEBTOON Unscrolled, a division of Wattpad WEBTOON Studios, Inc.
36 Wellington Street E., Suite 200. Toronto, ON M5E 1C7
The digital version of Cursed Princess Club was originally published
on WEBTOON.com in 2019. Copyright © 2019 by LambCat.

www.WEBTOONUnscrolled.com

No portion of this publication may be reproduced or transmitted, in any form or by any means, without the express written permission of the copyright holders.

First WEBTOON Unscrolled edition: January 2025

ISBN: 978-1-99834-141-2 (Hardcover)
ISBN: 978-1-99885-418-9 (Trade Paperback)

Names, characters, places, and incidents featured in this publication are either the product of the author's imagination or are used fictitiously. Any resemblance to actual persons (living or dead), events, institutions, or locales, without satiric intent, is coincidental.

WEBTOON, UNSCROLLED, and associated logos are trademarks and/or registered trademarks of WEBTOON Entertainment Inc. or its affiliates.

Library and Archives Canada Cataloging in Publication information
is available upon request.

CONTENT WARNING:
this graphic novel contains mature themes and
depictions of blood and violence.

Printed and bound in Canada
3 5 7 9 10 8 6 4

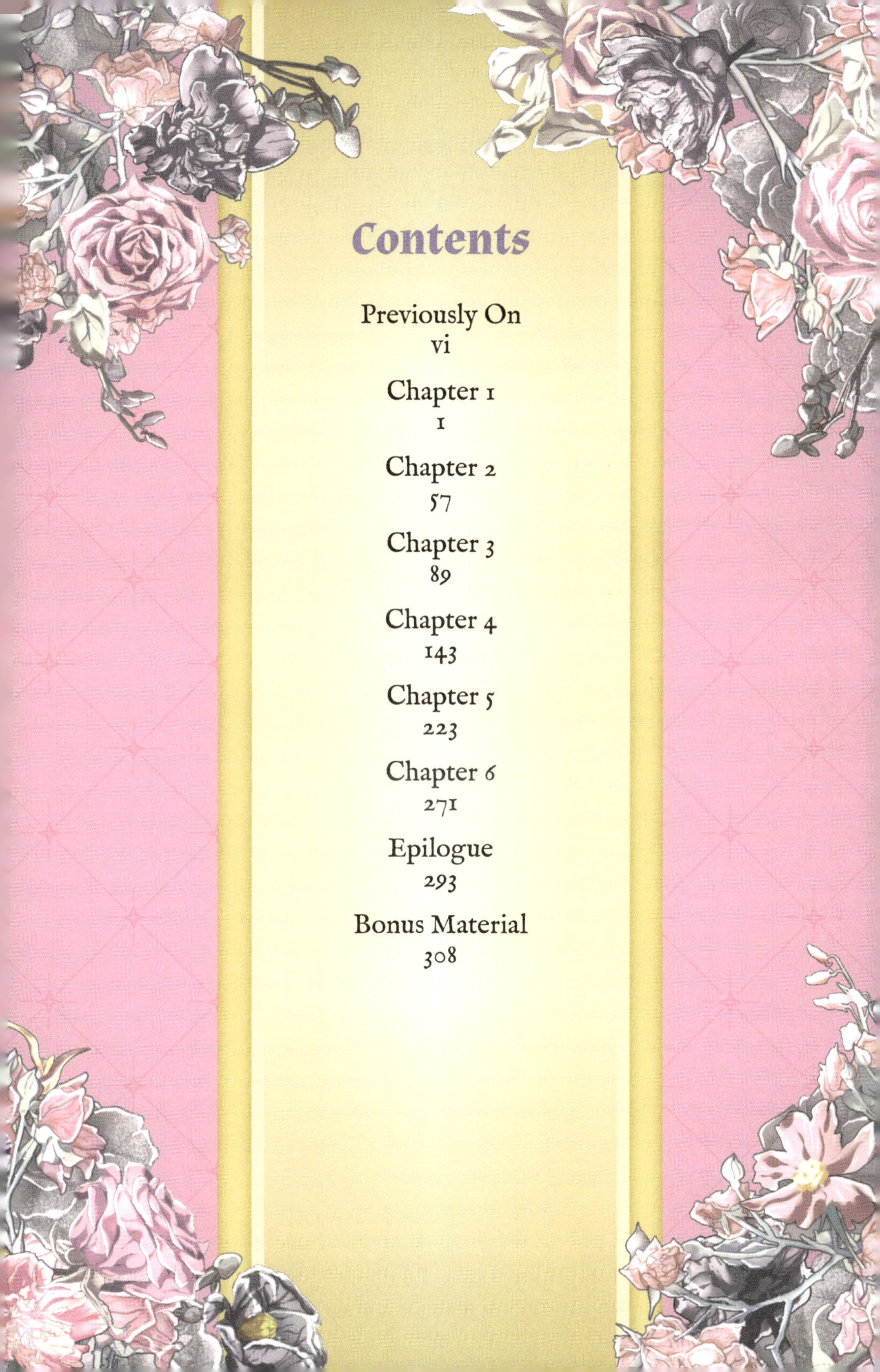

Contents

Previously On
vi

Chapter 1
1

Chapter 2
57

Chapter 3
89

Chapter 4
143

Chapter 5
223

Chapter 6
271

Epilogue
293

Bonus Material
308

Previously on CURSED PRINCESS CLUB...

The Pastel King has invited Lord Leopold to paint a portrait of Gwen. Leopold is determined to get closer to her, though Jamie attempts to sabotage him, leading to a heated feud between the two.

Frederick hears of this and embarks on a journey to visit Gwen and ask her to the Bippity Bop gala.

Prez tells the club that her spiders have detected a new cursed prince nearby to recruit to the club. Nell is overtaken with a terrifying premonition.

Meanwhile, Frederick meets Prince Whitney, who is still alive, though with a slightly new appearance. Whitney helps Frederick meditate and unearth his feelings for Gwen.

Frederick finally arrives at the Pastel Palace, and after a grueling art duel, tries and fails to invite Gwen to the gala.

Leopold finally finishes the portrait of Gwen and reluctantly realizes he doesn't hate Jamie as much as he thinks.

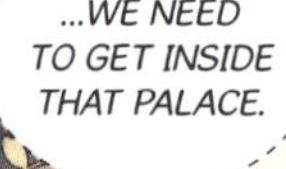

Last but not least, the CPCPCP. discovers the next step needed to uncover the mysterious truth about Gwen. But it seems that Nell's forewarned disaster is right around the bend.

Chapter
1

The following events in this volume take place over the course of one day...
knock
knock
knock
8:00 a.m.
Yes, come in!
CREEEAK
Princess Maria (age 18)
Good morning, Father—

Oh! I mean—
Good morning, Molly!
Sorry to startle you, Your Highness.
Your father is preoccupied this morning, so I'm waking everyone up today.
Preoccupied...?
pat
But Father never misses waking us up unless he's out of town on an expedition...

Hmm...
chirp
chirp
Don't mind me, though.
I'll just do my daily tidying up now and be out of your hair.
Go on now. Shoo!

Breakfast will be waiting for you downstairs shortly, Your Highness!
Thank you, Molly!
step
step
step

Well...
I do have a busy schedule today...

...so I might as well start my day as usual!
CREAK

FWOOSH~
I ♥ BLAINE
B
The Prince Blaine Trivia Book

Good morning, Blaine!!
Good morning, Schozart!!
"How did you sleep, my darling?"
I slept well, thanks for asking!
hahaha
Oops...!
slip
I get to go shopping in town this afternoon, so maybe I'll pick up a new dress for our next date!
B-BLAINE!!

It's a glorious day today.
Really? Looks like a crappy one to me.
It's gloomy and muggy. Kinda seems like it's gonna rain later.
No, you don't understand...
Remember how the king said last week that if no one was free to chaperone the princesses outside the palace...
a guard would get to do it?
Yeah? So?
Well, guess what happened earlier today in the guards' lounge?

Listen up, folks. I know it's not in our usual rotation of duties...
but the king needs one of us to escort his daughter into town.
Her mission is to...what does this say?
Buy some skincare...?
...So who wants to do it?
Oh, I could escort her. I love skincare.
Uh, sorry bro, but your damaged moisture barrier says otherwise. I think I'd be the better choice.
W-wait!! Which princess is it?!!
Hmm, let's see here...
Princess Maria.

M-ME! Give it to me!! I'm pulling rank as lieutenant!!
—And not just any lieutenant but the youngest one in the history of this squad!!
Cool your jets, kid. You're fifth lieutenant.
That's literally a position we made up to get someone to do everyone's paperwork...
and manage the lost-and-found receptacle for no extra pay.
WHATEVER!! I'M ESCORTING MARIA, YOU HEAR THAT?!!!
I DON'T CARE WHAT IT TAKES!!!
Pleeeease, I don't care what it takes. I'll do anything you want...
Whoa, whoa, take it easy, Beckett.
Excessive squinting causes fine lines.

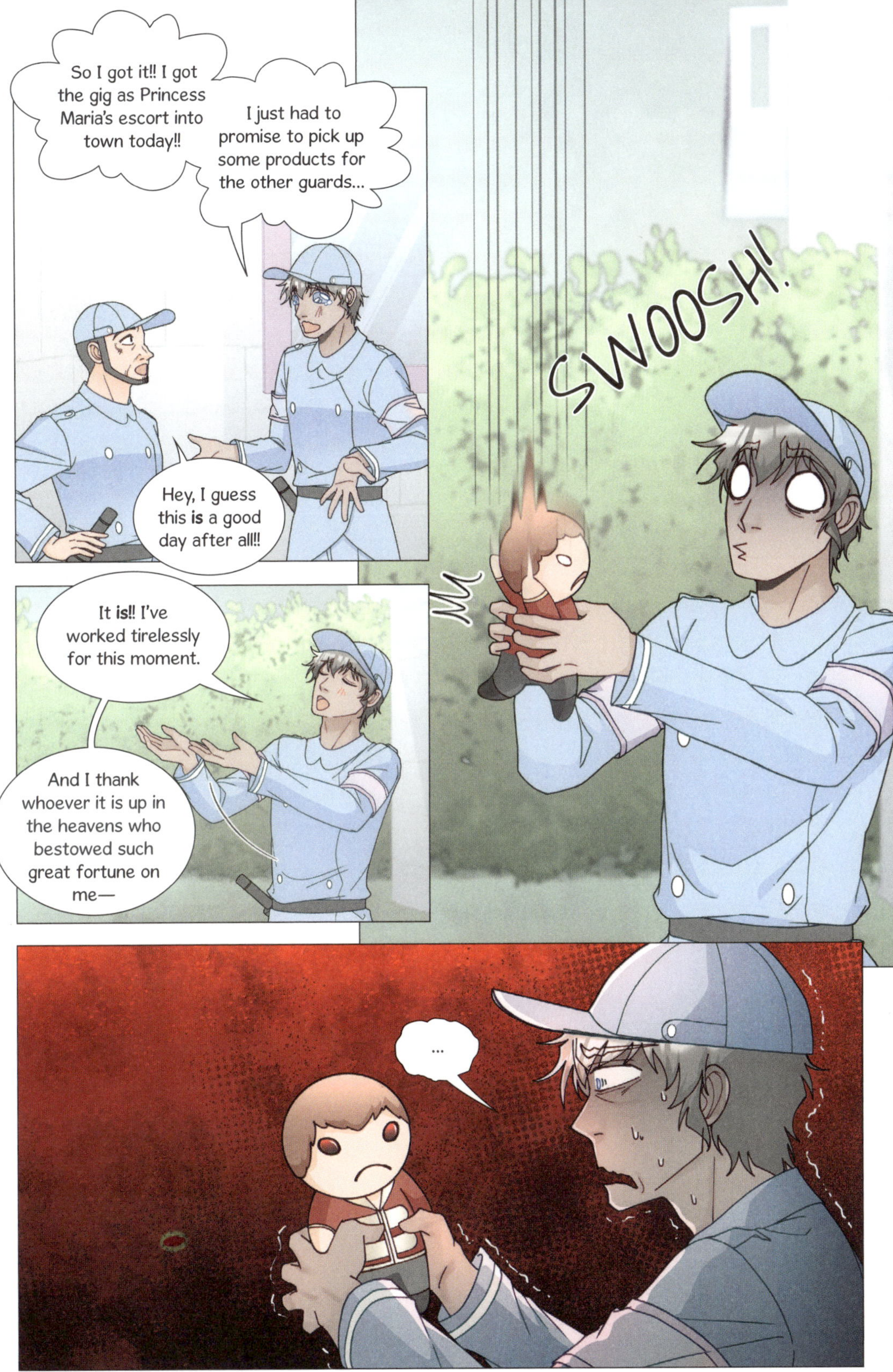
So I got it!! I got the gig as Princess Maria's escort into town today!!
I just had to promise to pick up some products for the other guards...
Hey, I guess this **is** a good day after all!!
It **is**!! I've worked tirelessly for this moment.
And I thank whoever it is up in the heavens who bestowed such great fortune on me—
SWOOSH!
...

Back inside the palace, Molly proceeded to visit the other siblings' rooms...
Morning, Molly! Where's Daddy?
Princess Lorena (age 17)

Hrrg...
...and carry out her daily cleaning routine.

Morning, Dad—!!
Prince Jamie (age 16)
AAAAH! I'm so sorry, Molly!!!
Don't worry, Your Highness.
I literally can't see a thing...

But Molly found she needed to rest her eyes for a while before she reached Gwen's room.

Z
Z
Princess Gwendolyn (also age 16)

I'm still seeing cracks in my reflection when I'm alone.
I've been making time to bake things for myself, but...
...I don't think it's helping much anymore.

I'm not sure what else I'm supposed to do...
We should all take more time to admire who we are right now, with all the pieces we've gathered so far.

I know that she means I'm supposed to stop thinking of my reflection as something I need to fix...

and to admire it as it is, but...

...that's kind of hard to do when this is all I can see of it.

Is there anything else I can do on my own...?

waddle~

Friends? In memories...and objects?
I have this ribbon Monika gave me when we were helping clean her room.
Gwen, please take this as my apology for almost smothering you earlier!!!
Th-thank you, but it's a little big for me to take home...!
H-how about if I just take this little ribbon?
So... if I tie this ribbon in my hair...
...it can help me feel a little more like...
Monika and the Cursed Princess Club are with me all the time?

I can't tell if it helped much, but...
I do kind of like it.
That's the book Frederick loaned me.
THE DOGYSSEY
"The Dogyssey...
"A tale of a dog who learns perseverance and other life lessons on his long and difficult journey to reach the one he loves.
Abridged and condensed for children who have no patience...?"
THE DOGYSSEY

I'm sad that Frederick couldn't visit for very long last week.
But I guess by the same notion that Leopold mentioned...

...maybe that's why I really enjoy the books he lends me.
Because even if we don't get to talk much...
THE DOGYSSEY

...I feel like I get to know him a little more each time.
THE DOGYSSEY

knock
knock!
—C-come in...!!
THE DOGYSSEY

Morning, Gwen!!

9:00 a.m.
Ugh, I ate too many eggs...
So no one has seen Papa all morning?
step
step

Nope...I guess he has somewhere he has to be this morning.
I hope everything's okay...

I'm more concerned about making it through class today.
yawn~
I just want it over with. I have some important shopping to do in town later!

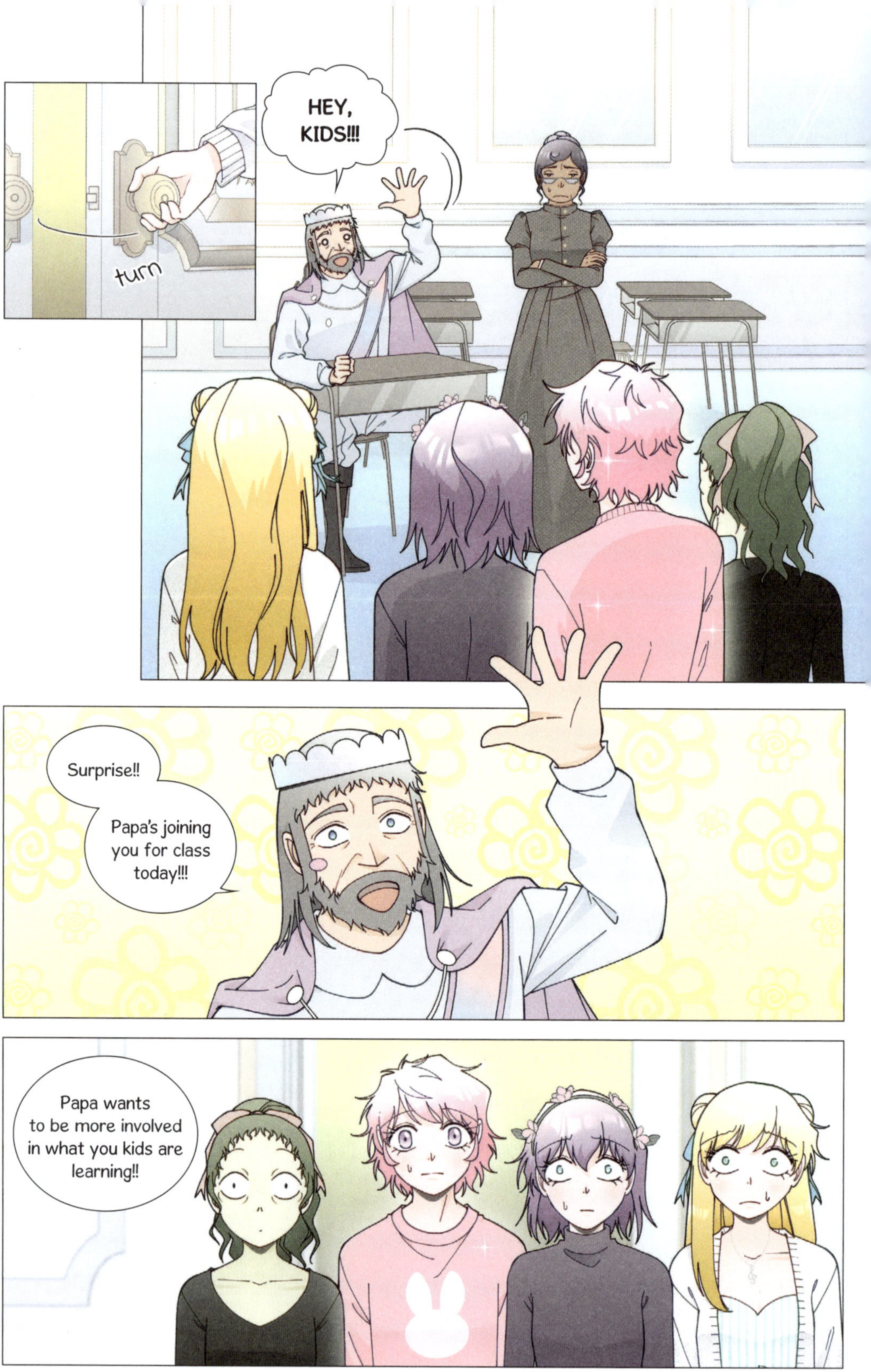

turn

HEY, KIDS!!!

Surprise!!

Papa's joining you for class today!!!

Especially you and your fancy princess school, Gwennie-pie!!
Papa wants to hear about everything!!

Yaaay school!!
Yaaay parenting!

Who doesn't love having their parents at school?! Yaay~!

Your Father.

Hey Dad~

WHAM!

Papa loves school! Let's learn lots of fun stuff today!!

And just like we discussed earlier, there will be no attempts this time to cut my lesson short with bribes of sugary treats.
Isn't that right, Your Majesty?
Yes, ma'am...
Wonderful.
Well, I'd like to start by having each of you give a little status update on your extracurricular studies.
I also hope you've all continued to think of ideas for your final projects.
Yes, Miss Agatha!

I came prepared this time!
We made a list of all the useful skills I've learned from the CPC without revealing too much about it!
Ooh, how about volunteering!
Um... decluttering skills?
Proper courting etiquette for two lobsters in love...

Besides...we did pressed flowers last week.

Did everyone make their bookmarks?

Umm, yeah... so for my food-critiquing business, we just passed the end of the third fiscal quarter.
I've got a profit-and-loss statement, balance sheet, accounts receivable aging report, and other documents for you to review, Miss Agatha.
...Huh?

Y-yes, very good. You can just, uh...leave those on my desk.
Maria, how about your studies?

It's going great! I'm working with my vocal coach to increase the projection of my voice so that I can reach more people with my concert next spring.
I've decided that I want to hold it in the middle of the Pastel Plaza, and—

Wait...the **Pastel Plaza?** B-but...that's **outside!!**
You're not possibly thinking of singing in town, in front of strangers, are you?!

Y-yes, Father. My dream is to inspire others with my voice...
so I want to sing directly to the people of our kingdom.
And since we're allowed to go outside now under your new decrees, it shouldn't be a problem—

Oh, it **absolutely** is a problem!! My decrees only allow you to go outside and engage in safe, preapproved activities!
It does not allow you to sing and expose yourself to the dangerous masses like a sitting duck!!
Your voice will be plenty inspiring enough when you sing your recital just for us, within the comfort and safety of our palace.

Besides, Miss Agatha would never condone any activity that put my children in such a dangerous position... **Isn't** that right?
O-of course, Your Majesty...
...

Yeah, it's honestly been really tough, Miss Agatha, and I could really use your advice.

Every time I try to learn about defense, I just remember the old adage that "the best defense is a good offense."

So then I just do more of that.

Hmm...it's not my area of expertise, but perhaps—

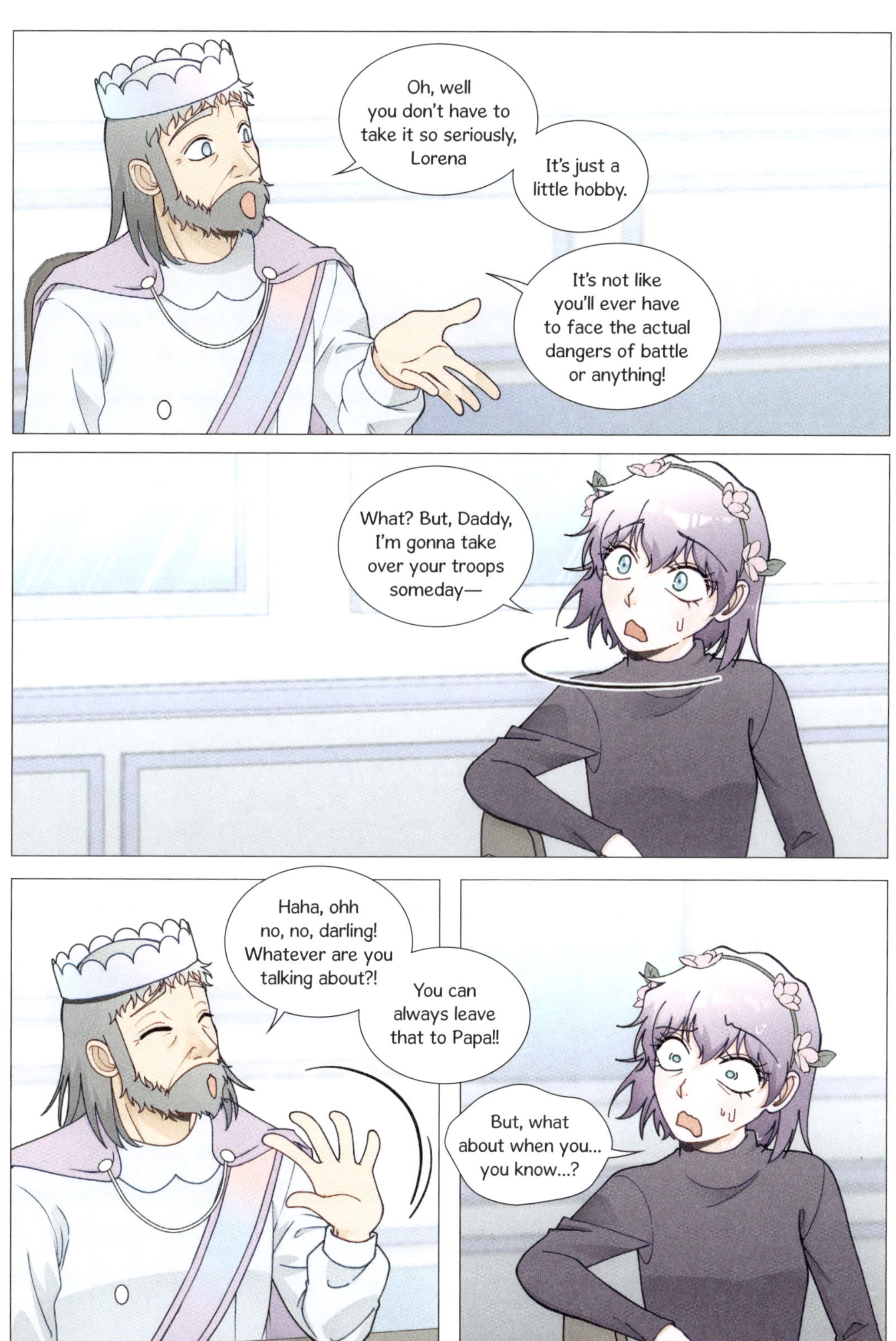
Oh, well you don't have to take it so seriously, Lorena
It's just a little hobby.
It's not like you'll ever have to face the actual dangers of battle or anything!
What? But, Daddy, I'm gonna take over your troops someday—
Haha, ohh no, no, darling! Whatever are you talking about?!
You can always leave that to Papa!!
But, what about when you... you know...?

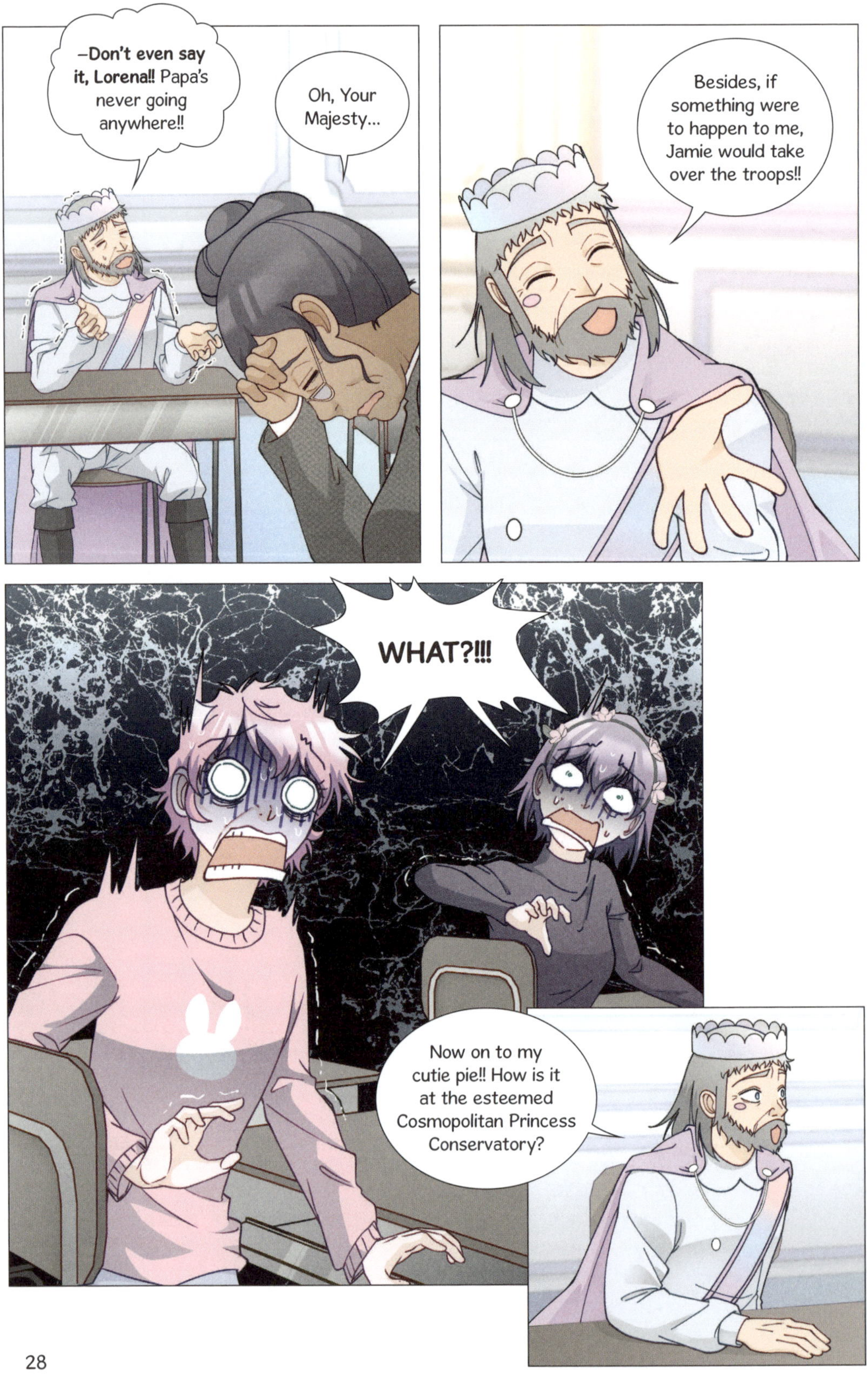

WHAT?!!!

Now on to my cutie pie!! How is it at the esteemed Cosmopolitan Princess Conservatory?

Oh no, Papa's on a rampage! I need to be really careful with what I say...!
Umm, i-it's been really great!
I've met a lot of amazing, inspiring princesses, and I've learned a lot of great life skills...
I-like volunteering and, uh, etiquette for...l-lobsters...?
Crap, these all sounded a lot better when we were brainstorming them...!
Ooh, lobsters?!
Are you going to prepare us a fancy lobster dinner someday?
–Lobster dinner?!!
...Well, I was actually thinking that for my final project, I could prepare a big dinner for our family and Miss Agatha!
But um... m-maybe not lobster...

Hey, now that sounds like something we can all agree on!
...Right, Your Majesty?
Yes! That sounds fantastic, sweetie.
nod
That wasn't too bad...!
sigh
But I have one change.
I demand you invite some of your teachers and classmates over too.
I wanna thank them for taking such good care of my daughter!
And I **won't** take no for an answer.

HUH?!!!
B-but...
but...
M-Miss
Agatha...
please...
shoot this
idea down!!
turn
You know what...
I actually agree
with your father
for once!
It would
be such an honor
to meet them and
compare various
pedagogies.

And I know. They're very busy, popular princesses.
So just ask them to choose any night they're free, and I'll clear my schedule!
I'll make sure this dinner **definitely** happens.
Thanks, sweetie! Great plan.
Uh-huh...
stretch~
Well, that was fun! Papa feels so much better about being involved in your studies.
Since that's all done, how about some frozen yogurt—
I heard that, Your Majesty!!
You **promised** you wouldn't cut class short—

Wait! Children, where are you going?! Class isn't over—
I'm having an existential crisis...
I need to lie down for a while...
I need to sneak down to the forest right now...!!!

Has anyone seen Monika this morning?

I feel bad for holding a meeting of the CPCPCP without her.

Hey, we need to focus right now.

I admit I wasn't really interested in this whole Gwen investigation at first.

But the fact that she's never seen a single portrait of her mother is straight up weird.

If we're gonna learn anything more about Gwen or her family, it's in that palace.

How are we gonna get in there, though?!

I told you. I have the perfect plan! We wait for the king's birthday. I'll hide inside a giant cake, and—

No.

For the last time, Syrah, this plan will not involve cake or seduction.

AAAAH!
GWEN!!
W-we can explain—!!

I'm sorry to interrupt, but I have an emergency!!!
Papa's demanding that the CPC come over to dinner at our palace!!

Uh...
What did you just say?

—I know! I'm so sorry. I've put the safety of the entire club at risk!!
But I wanted to let you know that I **ABSOLUTELY** won't let this happen.
I promise to take care of this myself—

NO, GWEN. WE **SAID**...

WE'RE HAPPY TO HELP.

gulp~

clench

11:00 a.m.

Ahem. May I have everyone's attention?

I appreciate you all gathering for this impromptu club-wide meeting.

I'd like to discuss a...**unique** proposition we've received this morning.

I can't remember...I kept repeating a phrase over and over.
That something was **"converging..."** What was it again?
I think it started with a *C*.
C-Cl...

Oh God...I think I kept repeating that "the **clowns** are converging"...
That sounds absolutely horrifying.
So I'd like to inquire if anyone would be up for attending a little costume dinner.
Costume dinner...?
What would we be dressing up as?

Uncursed princesses.
...Huh?

Gwen, would you like to take it from here?
U-um, sure...

So...as some of you know, Papa—er, the king of the Pastel Kingdom—
thinks that the CPC is some fancy, exclusive school for sophisticated princesses.
I have to host a dinner at our palace in order to show what I've learned here. And well...

...h-he wants you to come.

So Gwen needs a few of us who would be willing to disguise our curses and pose as classy, socialite princesses from her school.
As I'm sure you all can tell, it's an incredibly risky endeavor for everyone involved.
If handled improperly, it could get our club and Gwen in **a lot** of trouble.
But with that said...do we have anyone who wants to volunteer?
This is our chance to get into that palace and try to find a portrait of Gwen's mom!
Sure, count me in! All we have to do is eat your delicious cooking and act all fancy?
I can at least make my hand behave for that long—
HGNH— Okay...Maybe not.
Yeah! I'd get to drink your dad's fancy wine **and** lie?!
Those are my two favorite pastimes! Of course I want in!!
snap snap
Ooh, me too! I want to meet your family, Gwen!

Uhhh, oh boy...I appreciate the enthusiasm, everyone, but there are a lot of problems here.
Syrah, your nose will blow our cover the second you talk at that dinner.
Thermidora, no costume can hide your claws. And Saffron... this is a school for **princesses...**

Instead of asking who would be willing to volunteer, perhaps I should ask who would be able to volunteer... **convincingly.**
Maybe we should hold tryouts for this dinner, eh, kiddo?
nod

Well, if I don't pass the audition as a dinner guest, can I help behind the scenes somehow?
I'd like to assist as well, Miss Gwendolyn.
At the very least, I can share some tips I've learned over the years about entertaining for dinner parties.

Hey, it's not like we get invited to things every day. We're excited.

Besides, our reputation as your educators is on the line!

And if there's one thing we want your family to know about us, it's that the CPC knows how to entertain.

...Okay! Thank you, everyone! I feel like we can really do this!

I'll let Papa know. And he said he'll clear his schedule for whatever night works best for us.

Great. How about we do it after Nell's premonition passes?
We've added a ton of security reinforcements to the barn...
and I feel extremely confident that when I re-emerge from it in a few weeks after the new moon passes...
I'll have an empty stomach that'll be real hungry...
...to celebrate ZERO DEATHS!
ZERO DEATHS!!
Well, I guess I better start compiling a big shopping list of materials I need to get in town for this dinner!

12:00 p.m.

Okay, so according to Papa's newest decrees, if I want to go into town to buy materials...

I think I need to submit a written request for a chaperone.

Where do I do that, though...?

step

step

step

sob!

sniff

It sounds like someone's crying.

Is that coming from the music room?

CREEAK~

sob

whimper

Maria? A-are you okay?

Maybe later, when I've regained my voice a little.

Besides, you look like you're about to go somewhere, Gwen.

Huh? Oh, well, I was hoping to go into town, but I can do that later.

I don't even know how to request a chaperone—

Gasp
I totally forgot!!
I had a chaperone scheduled for a shopping trip into town right about... **now!!**
I get to go shopping in town this afternoon...
so maybe I'll pick up a new dress for our next date!
But I'm in no mood for shopping anymore...
Why don't you just take my place, Gwen?
You'll have to leave right now, though!!
I think I've kept them waiting outside!
Huh?! Um, okay...!

Princess Maria should be coming around the corner any moment now.
I can't believe it. I'm finally going to get to see the girl I'm in love with!!
Not that it matters to me what she looks like, unlike someone else...
You only like her because she's beautiful on the outside!
But I find her beautiful for who she is on the inside!!
Is my hair okay? Did I put on deodorant?
What else do I need to remember...?!
Sniff

The king has very clear rules for chaperoning his daughters.
Don't screw this up, kid, or he'll have **all** our heads.
You've been granted temporary permission to look the princesses in the face...
but you are **not** to speak to them, nor come within ten feet of them unless it's an emergency. Got it?!
I wouldn't dare screw this up!!
I'll be the most perfect chaperone Maria will ever have!
Gasp!
I think she's coming now!!!
step
step
Um, h-hi! I'm here to be escorted into town...?
I hope you weren't waiting too long!

That's Maria...?!
She's a bit... **different** than I imagined...
Is that really her?!
I don't think I'm allowed to ask...
You are **not** to speak to them, nor come within ten feet of them unless it's an emergency. Got it?!
How am I supposed to be sure, then?
Oh wait. I know!
Didn't Prince Blaine describe her in detail that one day...?

I like Maria **so much** that I'm gonna tell you everything you're missing out on, Lieutenant **Dandruff.**

You'll never see how beautiful her eyes are...

and how they shine, bigger and brighter than the largest ocean...

stare

Hmm....

*She **does** have really big eyes...*

in a bulging kind of way.

...?

What else did he say...?

You'll never feel the softness of her hair...
and how it wafts like a gentle spring meadow wrapped with ribbon...

There's the ribbon he mentioned too...
although her hair looks more **brittle** than soft...
Why does this guard keep staring at me without saying anything...?

And my favorite is how she smells...
like birdseed with a hint of slightly damp forest creatures...
Well...of course I won't try and smell her, but...

...?!

squint~

Bird... seed....

from Monika's ribbon

...Well, that all checks out.

But I'm still confused about one thing...

The person I'm in love with is the princess named Maria who sings from the balcony above my guard post.

She has a beautiful voice as bright and cheery as the sun.

Sometimes, in my peripheral vision, I'll accidentally catch a blurry glimpse of a girl with long, blond hair looking out over the ledge.

Is that not Maria...?!

inhale
There she is...
I've been granted temporary permission to look at them directly, and I have to know once and for all!
I **have** to see her sing!!
I HATE THE WORLD--!!
Croaky voice

Okay. Definitely not her.

Well...
if that's the case, then...

I'm so happy I get to chaperone Princess Maria, the love of my life!!!

step
step
step

Chapter 2

1:56 p.m.
Welcome to the
Pastel Plaza
I know that Papa ultimately just cares about us....
And he does try to make some compromises...
like how he's allowing us to walk into town now with a chaperone for our safety. But...
step
step
step
...I'm not really sure how **safe** this makes me feel!!
HEY! WATCH WHERE YOU'RE STARING, PAL!!
LEASH YOUR PET BEFORE IT ATTACKS SOMEONE!!
Sir, that's a street pigeon...
I've tried to walk up to the guard and tell him he doesn't need to be so vigilant...

...but for some reason, he keeps backing away at least ten feet from me!!

THAT ICE CREAM IS TOO COLD FOR HER PRECIOUS VOCAL CORDS!!!

Excuse me?!!

Um...Mister Guard?
Wait! Please don't back away this time!!
freeze!
Y-yes, Your Highness!
Um, I suddenly really, **urgently** need to go... uh...
do something **alone** right now, so...
Something urgent? Alone?
Oh—!
—O-of course!!
Please go right ahead, Your Highness!!!
I'll be waiting right here whenever you return!

He gets it! Thank goodness...
He's not so intense after all!
Th-thank you so much! I'll be right back.
turn

...
HEY!! GET OUT OF THE WAY, PEOPLE!
SHE'S NEEDS TO GET TO A BATHROOM URGENTLY!!
step
step
Note to self.
Write a letter to the chefs regarding Princess Maria's potential lactose intolerance.
I will prove that I can be the ultimate chaperone for her safety and digestive health.

And look what I found!

Someone left this box of free kittens to adopt!

I know I haven't completely cleaned my room yet...

but maybe Prez will let me take just one home!

Aaahhh, they're so cuuute!!

Never mind. I have to keep all of them!!!

nuzzle~

Oh...! That's really admirable, Monika!

But...maybe you could start with just one?

We have a cat, and all the responsibilities can really add up sometimes...

You have to feed them on time every day...

make sure they always have fresh water...

RAWRR!!

CAAAWW!!!

MONIKA—!!!

DASH!
...?!!
CAAAAAAAW~~!!
SCOOP
...?
sigh~

Don't worry. I've got you...

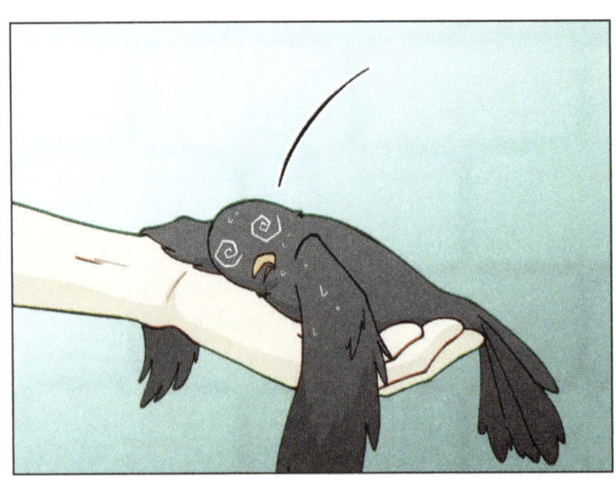

Th-thank you...!!
Um...about what you might have just seen–

It's okay. We all have our own quirks.
And it's nothing I haven't seen before—
step
step

Actually, wait. On that note...
have either of you ever seen someone here before who—

...?

What am I saying? Sorry. Never mind.
Have a nice day, ladies.
But that's ridiculous.
...!!
Poof!
I almost slipped and asked if those girls happened to have ever seen someone with a were-spider curse like Calpernia.
Most people with curses keep them a deeply hidden secret from everyone.
And there's no doubt she would have done the same.

Besides, I've searched every street of this kingdom over the last week...
and if she's here, she clearly doesn't want to be found.
I think it's time to accept the fact that she's not here after all.
I guess I'll leave and try some neighboring kingdoms.
step
step
Huh...The forest...
...!
pause

3:02 p.m.

Um...
I-I really appreciate you putting together this plan for me to ask Gwen to the gala...

But I thought we came to the conclusion that clandestine balcony serenades weren't such a good idea.

Okay, fine. The first one didn't go very smoothly. This plan is bulletproof, though!
Have some faith in your older brothers. Have we ever led you astray?
Uh, yeah. I almost fell off a cliff the last time we did this.
And last week you guys literally pushed me into a duel.

When I gave Gwen my book last time, and she found the ticket to the gala inside...

...she handed it right back as if even the thought of going anywhere with me could never cross her mind in a million years.

Well, that's why you need to sing your intentions to her loud and clear this time.
And just in case you lose your nerve again, Lance and I took the liberty of spelling out your proposal on a banner that we'll hold behind you the entire time!
Look—

?
QWEM
...What? Lance, what's with that banner? Who's "Qwem"?!
What do you mean?

Lance! Half of this sign is spelled wrong!
We can't use any of this now!
sigh~
Maybe we can salvage it though. Hand me that *G*...

GASP!
step
step

QWEM!!
I-I mean, Gwen!
I guess it's almost time for the serenade.
It's an absurd plan, but Blaine and Lance spent all this time planning it for me.
They're really trying to make me feel like a Plaid Prince alongside them...
But...I don't think any of this is actually what I want!
If I could just do what I wanted, I'd...I would...
rustle
I'M GOING TO TALK TO GWEN BY MYSELF!!!
What?! Frederick, wait!–
HGGHH—!!
Yank!

W-well, Your Highness, we've arrived back at the palace safe and sound.
I hope you have a very nice rest of your day....!

—MY NAME IS LIEUTENANT BUCKET DANDRUFF!!

—AAH!! I mean **Beckett Dandridge!**
My name is Lieutenant Beckett Dandridge!
I almost let that jerk fiancé of hers gaslight me out of my own name!!

step
step
step
Oh! Well, before you go, I just wanted to say...

Blaine's right. I need to start feeling more like a Plaid Prince!
I have the support of my brothers, I defeated Leopold in a duel...
Well, an art duel, due to a forfeit...
...and there's nothing left to stop me from going up and talking to Gwen right now!!

I wanted to say thank you for escorting me, Lieutenant Dandridge.

I know Papa must have given you really difficult orders to follow.

So, um, I got this pine-cone candle in town for you, if you'll accept it.

lift

Maria picked out this candle just for me?! That's so thoughtful...!

Oh no, I'm getting choked up. Hurry, before you start crying, tell her you love it!

...?!
faint

Oh God, my legs just gave out...
Who the heck is **this** guy?!! He's confessing to Gwen too?!!
I-I'm not up for fighting any other duels!!
...Retreat!

Is this what Leopold was talking about?
You're going to need a lot more grit to go after what you want, Frederick,
especially with Gwendolyn...as well as the formidable people surrounding her...

rustle
rustle
Blaine, Lance, h-help...! There's another—

—No, Frederick. We **DID** help!
We spent an entire week planning this elaborate serenade just for you!!
But you ran off selfishly and left me with nothing but this unsightly neck burn when you KNOW I'm modeling for a showcase of men's statement necklaces next week!
But it's fine. You don't have to follow the path your older, wiser brothers have laid out for you.
Like Father said, you're free to do whatever you choose.
But you **don't** get to have it both ways and cherry-pick our help only when things don't go your way!
So don't come back here until you've either manned up and talked to Gwen on your own...
...or unless you're willing to agree to do things our way—
the authentic, Plaid Prince way!!
Hmpf!
rustle

step
step
step
sigh
Give me a break...
Is it supposed to be this difficult to talk to the girl I like?!
It feels like there's always something standing in my way to make my life miserable.
Did I do something to deserve all of this?!
I thought that once I figured out what I wanted...
and pulled myself out of the hole I was in...
...I would reach Gwen, and everything in my life would fall into place.
Just like in that fairy tale.

Life's ruff!

How does that little guy find the strength to keep going anyway...?!

Deep down, I've always felt like a loser because I wasn't as impressive as my brothers.
I thought that if I could just be strong like them...
...or more popular like them, I'd finally be accepted. And I'd be happy.
THE OFFICIAL PRINCE BLAINE FAN CLUB
Wow...look at you!
I think Blaine and Lance need to watch out for you now!
But when I **did** finally get attention from people who had only ever noticed my brothers...
...it didn't make me feel the way I thought it would.
And the more I try to approach Gwen while holding on to this urge to be like them...
...the more horribly it all seems to go.

I just want to be myself with her.
...And that's not a feeling I've really had before.

But am I really going to turn away my brothers' support, after so many years of wanting it?
Sigh
I really wish I could ask someone for advice right now...

Wait. What would that Whitney guy say...?
Well, he'd probably tell some disgusting, oversharing story from his past.
But, after that...

...he'd probably tell me I need to sit...
and make some room...

Meanwhile, around the corner...
DID YOU JUST CONFESS YOUR LOVE TO MARIA?!
This is why you can't talk to her!!
Hurry up and take it back before the king beheads you!!

Hahaha, I didn't mean that! I jumbled up my words! How embarrassing!
Oh. That's okay, I do the same thing!
Well I should get going then, Your Highness!
Bye! Love you!
OH GOD! I JUST DID IT AGAIN!!
I'm so sorry, Princess Maria!!!
Stupid, stupid Beckett...
step
step

Maria...?
I feel sort of relieved to know I'm not the only one who messes up all my words when I'm nervous.
His job seems really stressful...

I know what I need to do!!

open

stand

Blaine and Lance, thanks for all your help, but I need to try to do things my way now!!

I need to complete my own Dogyssey, no matter what monsters I have to face...

starting with this guy right—

—Uh... where'd he go...?
Well that was easier than I thought...!
Maybe I'm actually a lot closer to the end of my journey!!
I'm gonna go talk to her now—
Ah, she's walking away! Wait...
step
step
She's not going inside her palace?

....?
step
step
step
step
step
Where would she be going right now with all that stuff?
check

step
step

Huh...? She's walking down ***there?!***
Into that forest that looks ***very*** clearly haunted...?!

Don't come back here until you've either manned up and talked to Gwen on your own...
or unless you're willing to agree to do things our way—
the authentic, Plaid Prince way!!

Well, I've already made my choice, and I don't want to back down anymore.
grip

So I guess...
step
step
Here I go.

Chapter
3

Whoa, what are you all wearing?

stretch

We're getting ready for our big auditions!

You know, to see who can pass as members of the CPC—

Yer, the **other** CPC. The fancy, un-cursed one.

What does their name stand for again?

I-it's called the Cosmopolitan Princess Conservatory...
But this all sounds great!
I'll just go inside to unpack these bags and gather a few things, and we can start when I come back!
I'm totally nailing the role of an uncursed, young, collegiate princess.
I just need to not lie for a few hours. Easy peasy...!
05
02
Oh yeah? What's the longest you've gone without lying?
Three days.
POP
'Kay, fine. Two.
02
Hmm, it's too bad Monika's missing out on this.
Also, where's Nell? She doesn't wish to join in on the auditions?
Um, dinner parties aren't really her thing...
Also, she said she didn't sleep very well last night, so she's napping on the couch inside.
03
04

So...what's your strategy for hiding your curse at the dinner party, Thermidora?
Oh! Well this dress has really big pockets! See? No more curse!
...S-sure, but...
03
04

I don't think I'll pass as a collegiate princess...
but maybe I could pass as a teacher at the school? Or a janitor?
Yeah, well, my curse makes me a shoo-in for a teacher!
I think I'd make a wise and dignified math professor.
01

Math professor?! You're fifteen.
Do you even know what an algebraic function is yet?
No, but I'll alge-**break** your jaw if you don't get back to work, janitor.
01

swing
haha
I'm envious, Abbi. I should be trying out for the role of professor.
At least I'd get to wear a pantsuit.
It's been a long time since I've worn a gown like this—

Psst...!
Oh! What's up, little guy? Do you have some new gossip?
We've spotted an intruder in the forest coming this way.
GASP!

Everyone, I need you to stay calm and listen to me.
The spiders have alerted me that an intruder is approaching us from the forest!
05
02
01

An **intruder?!** Headed us for **now??!**
Usually your spiders give us a way bigger warning when people have entered the forest!!
03

Yeah...! H-how did this intruder get past all of our security checkpoints so quickly?!
Well...we've never seen anything quite like it...
So then I tell Troy that if he's gonna dish it out like that, he better come with some receipts, and—
Hey guys... do you hear something weird?
Like distant screaming... but it's getting louder...
AAAAAAAAHHHH
SPLAT
We've never seen anyone just tumble all the way down the entire forest cliff.

But then he just stood right up...

...and started walking slowly toward the mansion!

Did you guys get a good look at this person?
Yeah, we did.
Tell us everything you saw.

whisper whisper

The spider says he had a... **plaid jacket?**

Plaid...
Huh...?
Waaaait a second...

During Gwen's slumber party.
My fiancé? He's a prince from the Plaid Kingdom...

Um, he has big green eyes and blond hair that kinda goes...like this...

And then it goes like... that way...?

...what?

whisper
whisper
And he has blond hair that...
That kinda goes like **this...?**
"Like a broom that dried at a weird angle..."

For each tear she shed...
...for each discouraging thought she had...
...and for each crack she sees in the mirror...
...we vowed to make him sorry for all of it.

Abbi, no.
Any violence we inflict on Frederick could jeopardize the safety of both Gwen and our club.
Since he's made it this far into our club, we have no choice but to let him in.
We're just gonna let him in? Are you out of your mind, Prez?!
This jerk's gonna find out about the Cursed Princess Club and where we live!
He could expose us all!!
What are you talking about, Abbi?
I think you've got the wrong CPC.
This is the Cosmopolitan Princess Conservatory.
We're just gonna start teatime a little early without Gwen.
and Frederick...
...can be our guest.

step
step
I have to keep moving forward.
I promised myself I would.
And I've made it all the way down here...
Though, sure, not in the smoothest way.
Ugh. Little Frederick was right.
Nothing good happens in this stupid, hilly kingdom.
But I saw her...
...just for a second, vanishing around the bend.

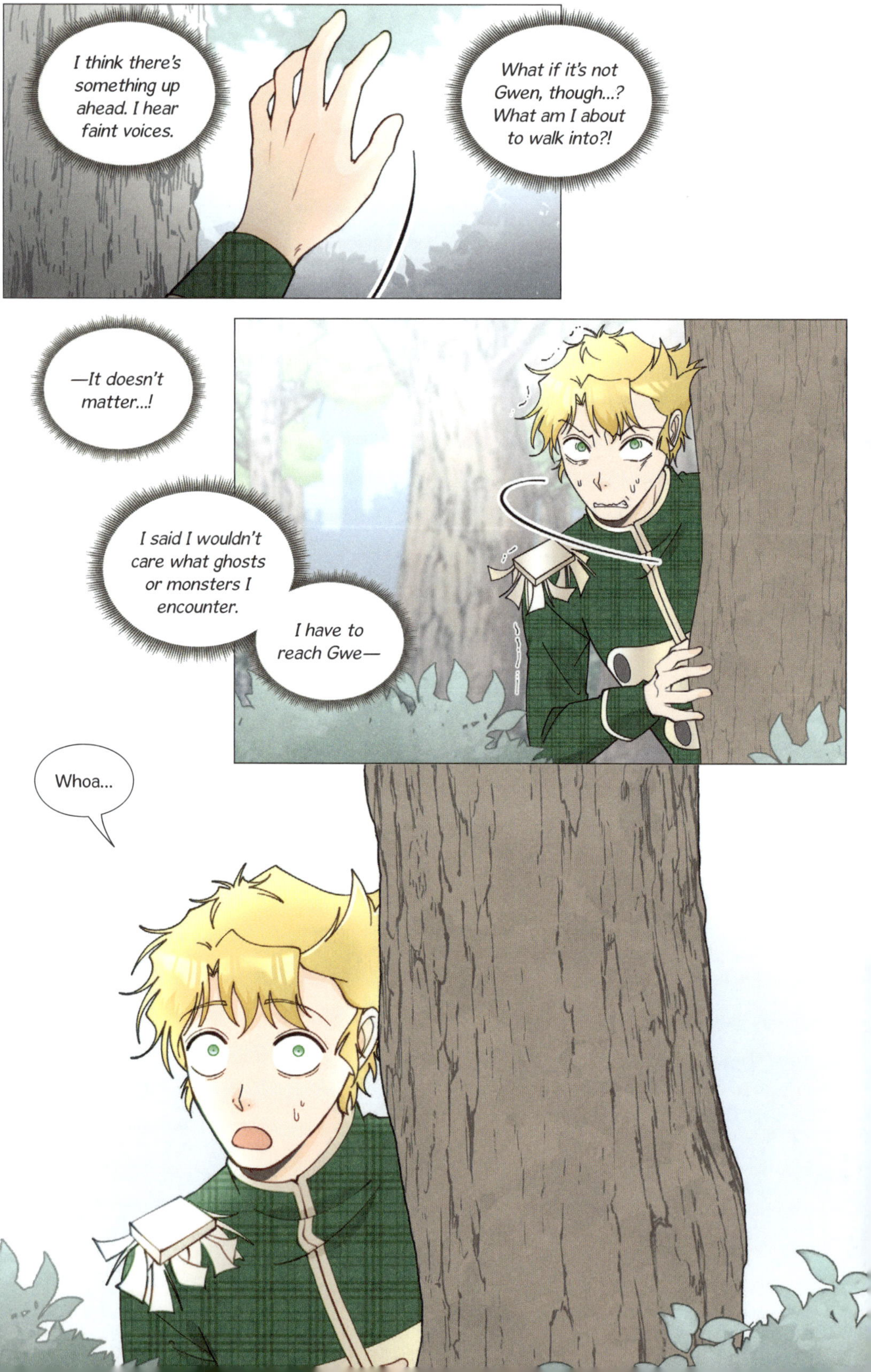

—It doesn't matter...!

I said I wouldn't care what ghosts or monsters I encounter.

I have to reach Gwe—

Whoa...

sparkle~
laughter
turn
Good afternoon...!
....Huh?

These aren't monsters, they're... **princesses!**
I really need to stop letting my imagination get ahead of me...

So that's Frederick, huh?

The crown prince of calling girls ugly in their own home...

That's a punchable face if I ever saw one...

Restrain yourself, ladies, and stick to our plan, as hard as it may be.

We have Curtis standing inside the mansion to intercept Gwen before she comes out.
He'll explain the situation to her.

Meanwhile, we just need to lure Frederick further in.
And since looks are so important to him, we'll put on our very best smiles.
Good afternoon, sir. What brings you to our humble institution?

U-um, I'm sorry, I didn't mean to intrude—
Wait...Did you say **"institution"**?

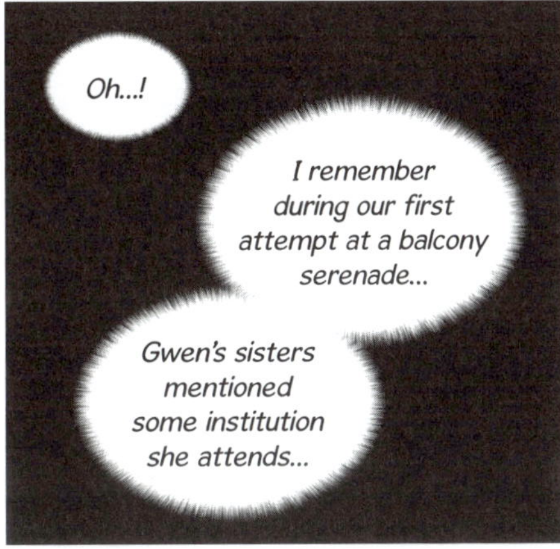
Oh...!
I remember during our first attempt at a balcony serenade...
Gwen's sisters mentioned some institution she attends...

Gwen gets an exception to leave home when she attends her fancy-pants elite princess school.

An artisanal school for princesses held at a mansion tucked away in some abandoned woods...?!
Hmm...That sounds on-trend, actually.

Come closer, sir. We won't bite.
Um, I'm looking for someone who attends your institution.
Her name is Gwen. I believe I saw her walk this way earlier?
step
step

Hmm, we don't know of anyone here named Gwen.
Do you know a Gwen?
Mumbles incoherently so as to not lie
Never heard of her.

...since you're here, why don't you join us for a little while?

Yeah! Join us, cutie~!

OPERATION ROYAL SLUMBER

This fake smile is kinda hurting my face, though.
I had so much more practice at it when I lived in my kingdom...
twitch~
Please have a seat!
As flattering as it is for these princesses to invite me, I want to focus on finding Gwen.
Um, thank you, but I'm going to try to inquire inside about school visitor policies—
I **SAID** HAVE A SEAT.

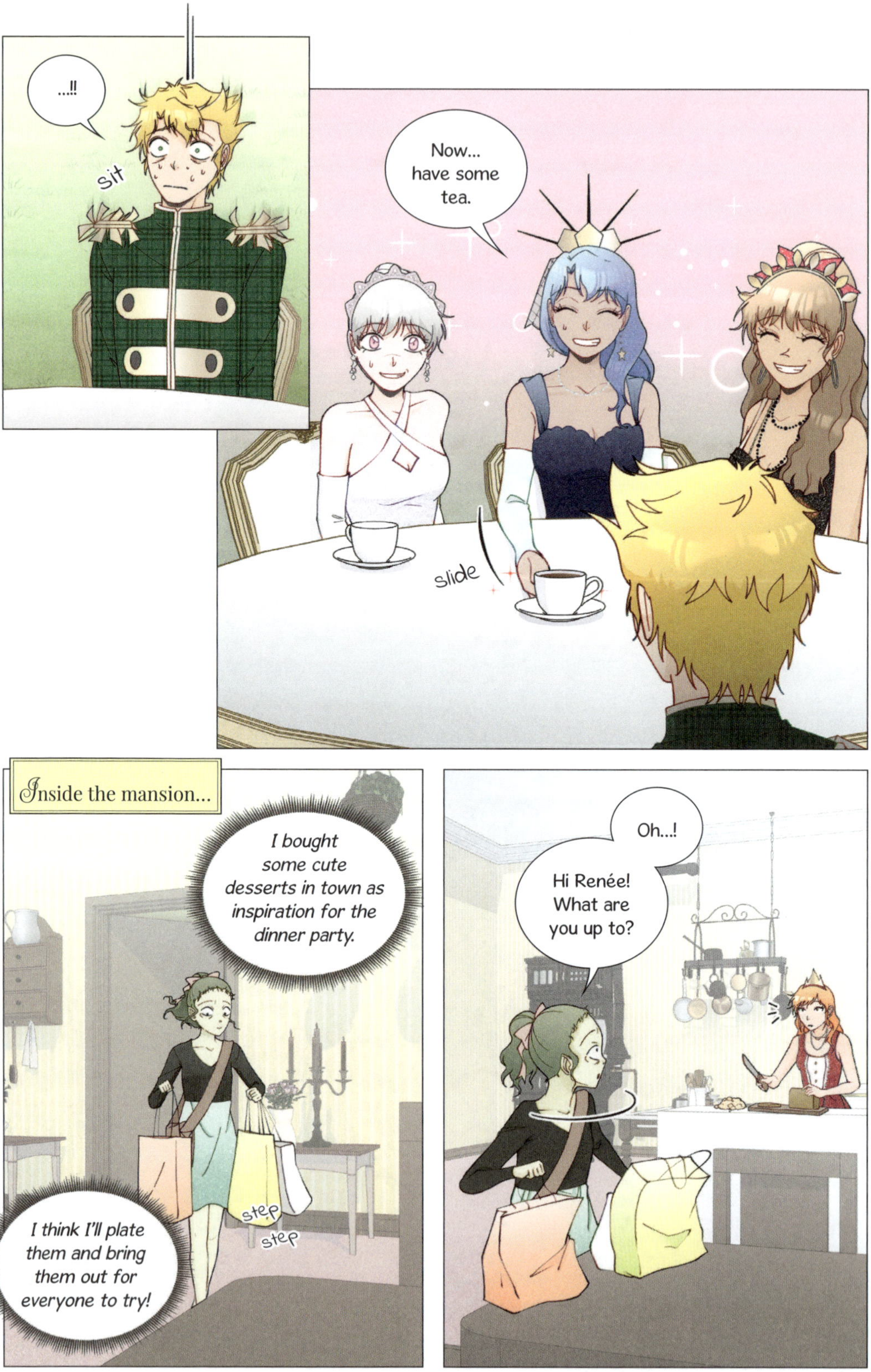

...!!
sit
Now... have some tea.
slide

Inside the mansion...
I bought some cute desserts in town as inspiration for the dinner party.
I think I'll plate them and bring them out for everyone to try!
step
step

Oh...!
Hi Renée! What are you up to?

Chopping up bread
to feed my swans
at the pond

That sounds really nice!
Oh...! That way the swans will be too full to eat the frogs she spits out from her curse...!

Um, actually... I've been hoping to get to talk with you.
I've been wanting to ask you about...

...Aurelia.

tick
tick
It was very generous of these princesses to invite me to sit down with them, but...
there's something a little...**unsettling** about them.
Like, I'm pretty sure that princess on the left hasn't blinked the entire time...!
Drink up! You haven't touched your tea...! Don't you like it?
O-oh! I'm just not very thirsty right now.
But it smells nice...! Very um, **strong...**

Please eat up, sir.
Uh... thanks.
So...what's this school like? I-is it any good?

ahem
Is the CPC... **any good?!**
clink
clink
Well, I think it's the best school in the world, **personally.**
It teaches many essential skills that most princesses never get taught...

...like how to wisely invest our finances...
how to properly delegate and manage our time...
...how to **CUT OUT** all the toxic relationships in our lives...
STAB!

Uh-oh...Prez is losing it.

I better take over before she blows our cover.

Uhh, so...what led you to follow this person named Gwen down here?

Yeah... What's your deal?

You **stalking** her or something?

I-I'm not a stalker!!

*...I guess that **is** what I did, though...*

I'm Gwen's fiancé! —Er, **was,** at least...

Oh! How quaint. I had a fiancé once.

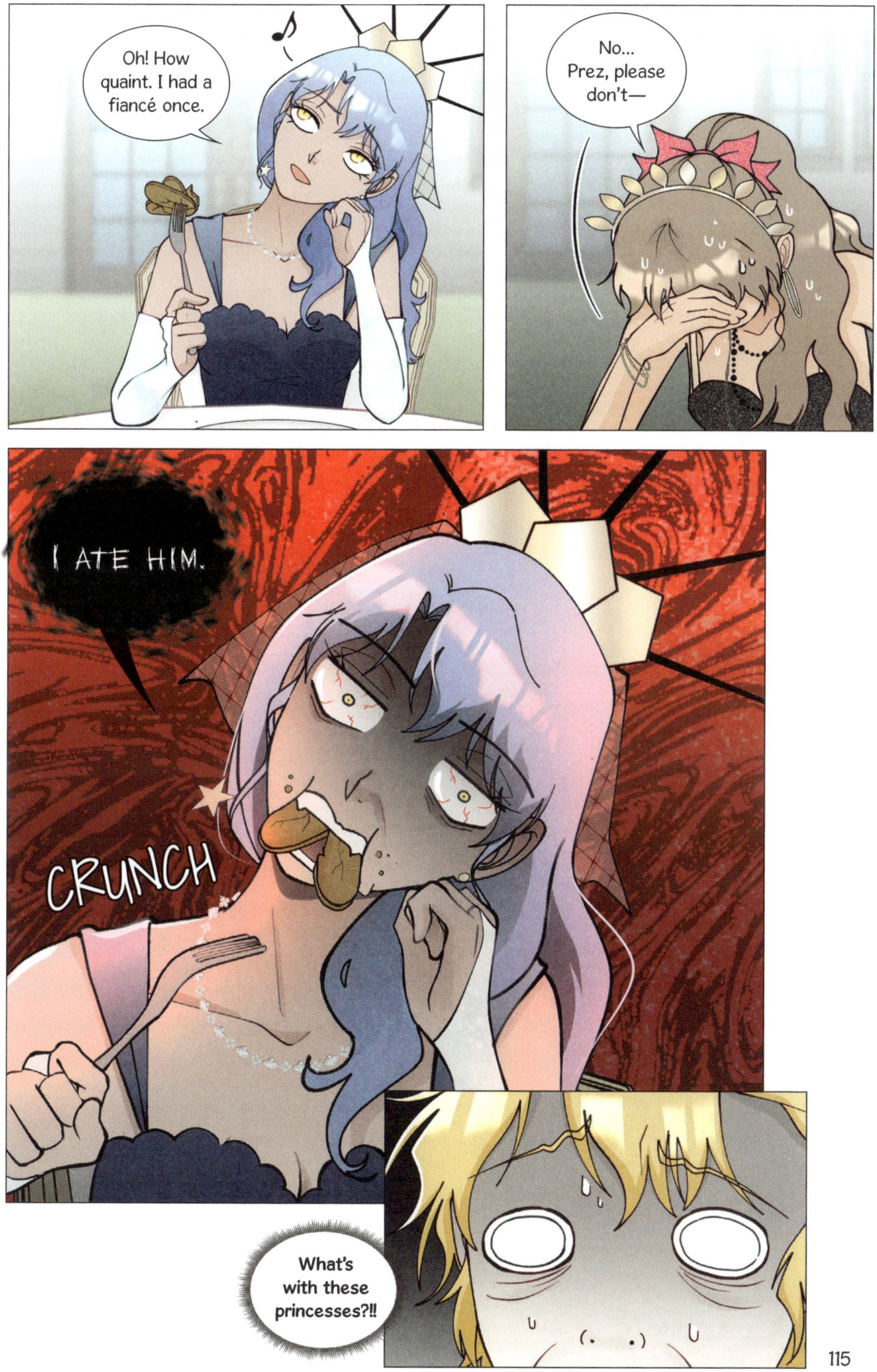

No... Prez, please don't—

I ATE HIM.
CRUNCH
What's with these princesses?!!

It might be my imagination again...
...but the mood here seems really heavy...!
munch munch
Maybe this isn't the right way to reach Gwen at all...

We need to knock this jerk out and toss him out of this forest forever...
And if he won't help us by drinking that tea...
...then maybe he'll like a taste of this teapot—

Wait...he's gonna leave on his own? Is that allowed..?!

He doesn't think Gwen is here.

And he said he doesn't know how he got down here...

W-well then...

Leave it to us!!
We'll escort you back up so fast it'll all be a blur!!
—WHOA!!
dash—!

U-um, thank you!
I-it was really nice meeting you all!!
Yeah, yeah, you too!!

GROW~
Aw, COME ON!!

step

WHOOOA!
RIIPP~

YANK!
AAAAH!!
What's going on back there...?

SMACK!
OOF!

thud

Ow, what happened...?
turn

WHAT THE...?

AAAHH!! IT'S OKAY, I'LL FIND MY OWN WAY OUT!!

CRACK!

Huh—?!!

thump!

Why leave so soon?

We're just starting to get to know each other a lot better, **Frederick.**

AAAAAAAGHH!!!

...

stop

Oh...thank goodness.

sigh~

But I **will** if that's what it takes to make sure you don't tell anyone about this place.

It's my utmost priority to protect the princesses in our sanctuary...

and you seem to have a real problem keeping your thoughts to yourself.

H-huh?!

Yeah, I wasn't gonna hurt you.
But I am gonna let this hand scare the crap out of you.

Well, not me. I got a hot knuckle sandwich just for you, Freddie boy.
crack

Why is the little old lady the scariest one?!!
AAAAAH! W-WAIT!—

Alert! Alert! There's someone in the forest!!

drop

Yeah, yeah, we know! We got 'em right here!

Thanks, buddy. You guys can take it easy now, okay?

No—

No one ever listens to me...

turn

So I bought it, a-and I was thinking maybe some of us could write her something and check in...!
...
I feel like she really misses you and the club.
A-and I'm fine if that happens to be why you're mad—!
Um...are you still angry about what happened?
nod
scribble
scribble

Oh...What is it?
That's not it.

scribble
scribble
I don't really know. It's hard to write into words.

Oh, well, it's okay! I didn't mean to—

W-WAIT!!!

How do you know my name?!!

Of course we know your name, Frederick.

We know everything about Gwen because we're her **real** friends. Unlike **you.**

Honestly, you've got some real nerve thinking that just being chummy with her will atone for everything you've made her go through.

We know **all about** how you feel toward Gwen.
Yeah.
And you know what? She doesn't need you in her life.
Y-YOU DO??!!
They know I like her?!

Gwen has more people waiting to love her than you can even imagine.

Even more people than that guard and Leopold?!!

And it's too bad for you because you're **really** gonna miss out on someone as wonderful and kind as her.

So just leave her alone, stop wasting her time, and—

EVERYONE NEEDS TO STOP TELLING ME WHAT TO DO!!
You won't make me drop my feelings for Gwen...
and you won't stop me from asking her to that **stupid gala** today!!
Uh...
What...?
Uh-oh...
D-did we make a huge mistake...?
Huh...well, I handled this all really poorly, didn't I?
Yeah I feel really bad...
I guess he's not a jerk. That's kinda sweet actually...

POOF!

Hiya, guys! Sorry I was gone for half the day!

I just had a really fun time in town and—

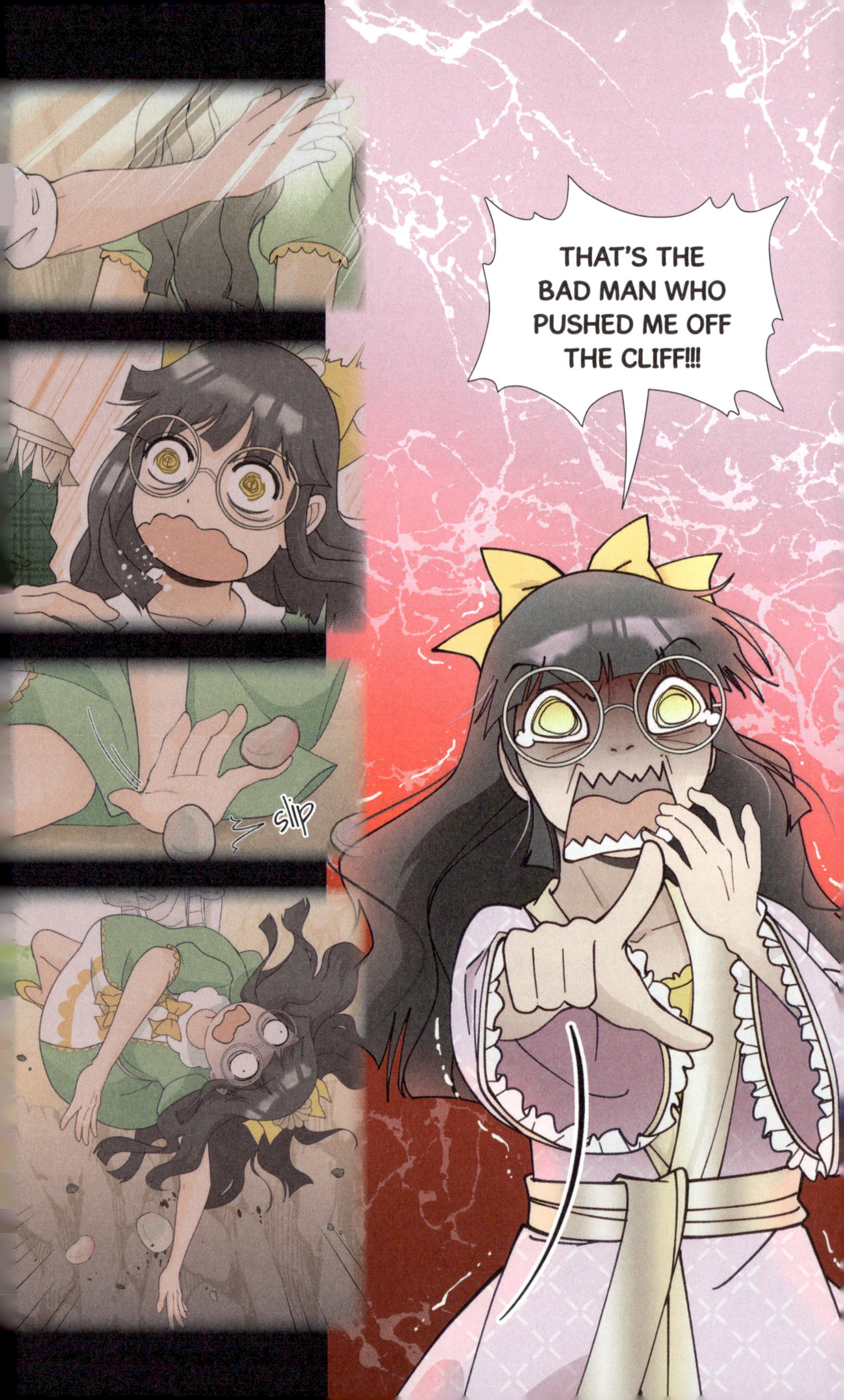
slip
THAT'S THE BAD MAN WHO PUSHED ME OFF THE CLIFF!!!

...cliff...?

pat
But I was sure it was Gwen who I pushed off that cliff...

He's not a jerk...
HE'S A MONSTER!!!
AAAAH!!! WAIT—!!!
CRASH!
freeze
step

F-Frederick...?!
What's going on here?!

Oopsies.
Gwen!! Um, we can explain—
Gwen—
THUD!

rustle
rustle
Pardon me...
snap!

Who's there?!

—Calpernia...!
I...found
you.

Uhhh, Prez?!
Hello?
What's with this other stranger in our forest now?!!
Do you know this guy?!!

Oh! I know him!
He's the nice, giant man from town who saved me!
Wait—**you** know this guy?!

He **is** nice. He taught me how to meditate—
Hey!! No one asked you, pal!!
Wait...

Did you just say that you know him too?!
Who **is** that guy...?!

drop
It's...

It's Prince Whitney...
of the Monochrome Kingdom.

Chapter 4

WARNING

This chapter contains
some blood and violence.
Reader discretion is advised.

Oh! I didn't notice Nell asleep on the couch!

I-should be quiet...

Clouds... converging... flash...

z z z

Miss Gwendolyn!!

We have an emergency happening outside.

groan

But please listen to me carefully, and I will explain everything.

Emergency?!! What's going on?!
Well...it may be faster if I simply show you.

GASP!

...Curtis?

What's the matter? Is everyone okay—?!
creak
CRASH!

F-Frederick?!!

...?

The emergency outside was **Frederick?!**
dash
I-is that Gwen? Or have I passed out now?

Frederick! What are you—
—I like your ribbon! It looks nice on your head...
all three of them...

H-huh? My ribbon?
Thanks, I...

...I like it too.
That's right... This morning was the first time in a while where I...

...kind of liked what I saw in the mirror on my own.

—Ah! What I meant to say was...

What are you doing down here, Frederick?!

shake

Oh, I saw you walking into the forest. And when I tried to catch up to you...

I tripped all the way down and just sort of ended up here...

Oh my gosh!! Are you okay..?! Your head looks injured!!

—!!!

U-um, no, that's not from... er...

...I-it's not so bad actually.

Prez!!
What's up with you right now?!!
And who's this other dude in our forest?!!
It's Prince Whitney...
...of the Monochrome Kingdom.
THE PRINCE...
...OF THE MONOCHROME KINGDOM?!

Really? That guy's a **prince?!** Huh...
That guy's **Whitney?!!**
As in the Whitney...

...Prez **killed?!**

dash-!!

slide-

She saved us all and created the Cursed Princess Club to protect us! And now it's our turn!!

So if you want to kill our president—

N-no, I—
You'll have to get past all of us first.
Starting with me.
Cursed Princess Club...?!
Wait, then...

I...I didn't kill anyone...?

Thank goodness...

Thank goodness I didn't kill anyone...

...

Calpernia...
She still has the same elegant but fragile sadness I remember from years ago...

I...
step

grab

I don't know how you're still alive.
But if you take one more step toward my club...
...I **will** kill you without hesitation or remorse this time.

...!!
I couldn't have been more wrong.
Even though she looks the same...

...it's like she's a completely different person.

So...Prez has just been wearing a weapon on her head this entire time?
Ah, that was our first craft project upon starting this club.
It's a carbon steel replica of her crown with detachable components for the ideal, discreet backup weapon.

Wait. I'm not here to hurt anyone...!
I'm only here to apologize to you, Calpernia.

Apologize?
Yeeeah, I'm not the same weak little pushover I used to be...
so you're gonna have to try harder with your lies.

They aren't lies.
Since our last encounter, I've come to realize just how many horrible decisions I made in my past that I can't take back.
Yeah. Clearly. We can all see your face tattoo.
Seriously, what's up with that...?
I-it's not a tattoo...
These are tiger stripes from a curse—

AAAAH! I see it now!!
He's not a zombie, he's a **were-tiger!!**
He gave himself a curse like Prez's!!!
Wait, tonight's a full moon too!!
He's gonna transform and kill us all!!
PREZ!! You need to transform and battle him! **Hurry—!!!**
RAWRR~
IT DOESN'T WORK LIKE THAT, SAFFRON!!
I can't just MAKE my period start whenever it's convenient!!
Right. Sorry.

Erm, it's not a were-tiger curse...!
It's just a tiger curse. But this was as far as it got.
I-I don't transform or have any powers.
—I mean, other than frightening animals and maybe having a few heightened senses.
Actually, that's how I came to find you all.
It was thanks to your screams, Frederick, which I was able to follow.
Y-you're welcome...
I'm happy to tell you more if you'll grant me time to explain everything and apologize to you.
I don't need whatever apology you may have.
And I don't really care about your curse.
But there's one thing I **need** to know, no matter what.

How...
...How did you survive?!

If you can answer that, I'll listen to what you have to say.
But the second you move from where you're standing...
I'll make sure they're the last words you ever speak.

Curtis, check him for weapons and take his belongings.
Yes, Your Highness.
step
step

Everyone, take a seat and listen.

And that includes you too, Plaid boy!
I'm a little busy now, but I'll figure out how to deal with you afterward!!
Ahh...!!

Frederick...
Th-they didn't hurt you, did they?
Huh? Oh, just this small scratch! And I think that was on accident.
They were mostly just **really** scary...
Hmm...
I guess I had a similar experience when I first ran into them too.
But if they did anything to you, I—

N-no, it's fine.
I don't really understand what's going on, but...
...I get that this is, um, a secret place that's really important to everyone here.
And to you too. Right?

Um...yeah. It is. They're really overprotective, and they can go overboard sometimes, but...
they're also really kind people who have helped me in a lot of ways.
So, um...I'm really sorry that you have to stay here for a while longer.
But i-if there's any way I could beg you to keep this a secret too—

Oh...! I promise I won't tell anyone...!
That's easy. No one talks to me anyway...

And, well, I wasn't going to leave regardless.
I'm actually pretty invested in hearing more about this Whitney guy.
Besides...

I'd really like to talk to you afterward about something, if that's okay.

Um, sure...!

I did it...!

Psst, hey, Syrah. Since we're having story time again...
do you think Curtis will make us some popcorn?
I feel less nervous when I nosh....

I-I wouldn't ask him right now...
Okay...

I think Prez's spiders just gave up on security for the rest of the day...
rustle
rustle
step
step

The pretty llama from the portrait!!
Are you here to comfort me and be my new pet?!!
shake

Laverne...!! Did you change your opinion of me...
and come here after you heard my screams too?
step
step
Hmmm....

step
step
It wasn't quite Frederick who Laverne changed her opinion of...

smooooch

4:23 p.m.
Everyone gathered and sat down to anxiously listen once again...
...to a story that took place several years ago in the Polygon Kingdom.

...But this time, it was from a different point of view.
Well... as you know, Calpernia...

When our marriage was arranged, I was elated.

With the eldest princess of the Polygon Kingdom as my bride, the scales would finally tip in my favor, and my father would choose me as his successor once and for all.

When I attacked Asa with the cursed serum in order to transform him into a house spider...

...I was shocked by your devotion and selflessness when you jumped in front of him.

But not as shocked as when you instead turned into a giant, ferocious were-spider.

After this terrifying transformation, your newly cursed form immediately descended upon me in a bloodthirsty rage.
And though I was no stranger to gruesome sights...
I froze in absolute terror and saw my life flash before my eyes.
The life I saw was awful.
It was lonely and bitter, consumed by a never-ending, unfulfilling thirst to compete, to win, and to dominate.
And what did it all amount to?
Nothing. I lost.

DASH-

HEY!!

CHOMP!

SNAP OUT OF IT!!

AAAAH!!

yank

—Whoa,
whoa...
Are you trying to say that the reason you're alive...
...even though I have a hazy memory of biting off your head...
...and even though I spit out parts of your earrings and tie...
...is because Asa saved you?!

N-no...But that still doesn't explain everything from the next morning!
I definitely ate you!!
There was blood everywhere, I felt sick, my stomach was completely bloated, and—
...
...oh...
....Oh.
Well...the night wasn't exactly over yet either...

Are you okay?! Are you hurt anywhere?!

pant pant

Did this twerp I tried to murder just save my life?!

I-I'm fine...

Good, because we'll need all our health to make it out of this room alive and get help for Calpernia.

We're safe for now if we stay quiet and hidden in the shadows.

TIC TIC TIC

But we'll need to create a distraction for her, and then we can run toward one of the two exits.

A distraction, huh...?

GRAB
Thanks for volunteering, then, you stupid try-hard!!
WHOOOA!!!!
Ugh!
THUD
Oh, shoot...

Calpernia!!
This is all my fault!
I'm so sorry!!!

I have to reach
your parents so they
can help you, though,
so please don't kill
me yet!!

An air
vent...?!

...?
slide
She's retreating...?

I hear her running away toward something else...
TIC
TIC
TIC
TIC

AAAAAAAAGH!

The Monochrome Prince!!
Where is he?! I can't see anything!!
grab
I can't sit by and let him die out there, even if he IS an awful, sexist attempted murderer...

RATTLE RATTLE
What?! No...!! Why isn't this opening from the inside?!!
AAAGHHHH!!

Ugh...I was so close to reaching the exit.

But I just **had** to turn around and retrieve my crown...

And of course, **now** this stupid woman decides to hold me down when I'm trying to leave.

spin
Oh my GOD, is that stuff coming out of her butt?!
She's gonna wrap me up in a web to eat!!
I gotta get out of here!!!
How, though?! It's taking all my strength to push her back.
Instead of pushing...
—That's it!
HHRRGHH-
COME HERE!!
YANK!
KICK!

SLAM!
I barely managed to break loose...
dash
tip
toe
...and slip out of the Polygon Palace unnoticed...

So...
I-I really didn't kill anyone...!!
Yaaay! you're not a murderer!
pat pat
Curtis, can we get that on a cake?

As soon as all threats in the forest are resolved...
I shall whip up my signature chocolate ganache.

Hold your horses, everyone.
If you're not dead, then why didn't news ever reach Prez?
And also, **what** is with your face?!

I can answer that if you'll listen to my story just a bit longer.

After limping out of the Polygon Palace, I somehow managed to claw my way back home to the Monochrome Kingdom.
It took me two excruciatingly long days, and I was exhausted, famished, and heavily injured.
As I walked into my palace, I was ashamed and scared to see how my family would greet me in my state of failure.
limp
I-I'm home...
WHITNEY!!! Thank goodness you're alive!!
You're hurt, though...! Here, lean on me.
H-huh?! What are you doing, Greyden?!
And what do you mean "you're alive"?!

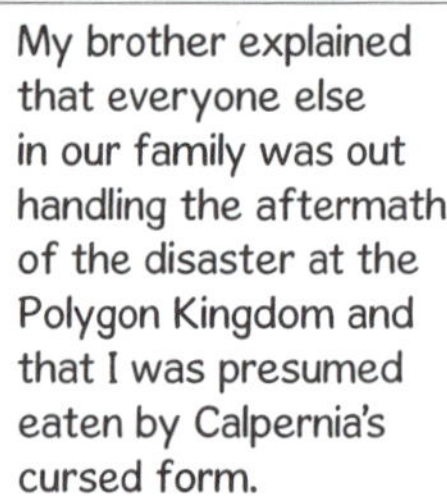
My brother explained that everyone else in our family was out handling the aftermath of the disaster at the Polygon Kingdom and that I was presumed eaten by Calpernia's cursed form.

Whitney, news of your death made me realize that I'm tired of always competing with everyone. Especially you.
At least while our parents are gone, can't we just stop and celebrate your return in peace...?
I...I'm tired too...

Okay, well then first let's get you to the infirmary!
My injuries are fine for now, I really need sleep though.
And food...
step
step

O-okay! Well then take a long rest, big brother.
And when you wake up, I'll have a big feast prepared for you.
Sure. Whatever...
If I had not been delirious from exhaustion and blood loss...
I would have realized that there was no way my little brother could be happy to see me alive.

When they received an urgent message from the Polygon Kingdom of my supposed death, it practically secured his place on the throne.
So the instant he saw me walk through the door, he started scheming for a way to make sure I truly died before our parents returned home.
And it turns out... we siblings really think alike.

Lemme guess, you got stabbed with a needle containing a cursed serum too?

Th-that wasn't **quite** my brother's style.

He chose the less barbaric plan of slipping it into my wine glass over dinner.

But, I mean, spiking someone's drink is obviously a disgusting, inexcusable action that only a horrible person would ever do...

...and turn him into a pelt for me to wear at my coronation.

Um...Your Highness, with all due respect...

Why don't you turn him into something else monochrome, but smaller and less... **deadly?**

...Like a dalmatian?

WHAT KIND OF **FREAK** WEARS A COAT MADE OF DALMATIANS?!!

Now hurry up and get out of here!!

My former servant ended up returning to the same black market I sent him to...
How can I help ya again, ol' man?
M-May I purchase another cursed serum...?

Sure thing. You want a frequent customer card?
Yeah, okay.

TIGER
And with that purchase, my little brother's plan was all set.

Servant...
it's time. Go wake up my dear brother and tell him that...
...dinner's ready.

4:50 p.m.
rustle
Everyone continued to listen quietly to the conclusion of Whitney's story.

I can't believe this is the same guy that offered me tea and taught me a way to calm my negative thinking.
He tried to **kill** someone?!

My brothers were right.
I **should** be more careful about strangers I meet and spend the night with...

So after I returned home and awoke from much needed rest...

Ugh, I'm starving. What's for dinner—
step
step
Oh.
Uh, this is a lot fancier than I thought it was gonna be.
Are you wearing a **tuxedo?**
Well, of course I am! I want to celebrate that my big brother is alive and well!!
Look, for tonight's feast, I've had all your favorite foods prepared.
Which is mostly meat...
So come in, Whitney! What are you waiting for?
It **does** smell really good...
step

Before we begin, I'd like to make a toast.

Here's to a new era of peace and camaraderie between siblings.

...

I wouldn't mind that...

Cheers.

Welcome home, Whitney.

clink

sip
So drink up, Whitney...

PFFFTT!

SPUTTER
COUGH
Ugggh, it went up my sinuses...
WHAT?!
Why did you spit it out?! Did you taste the curse?!!

No, I spit it out because you're pairing a Riesling with venison, you ungodly pleb—
......
...Wait, what did you say—?

AAAGH!!
clank
Wh-what is this...?!
GROW
Yes...it's happening!!
What's the matter, Whitney? Cat got your t—

Oh. I think it stopped. I'm okay.
What?
...But I've been waiting all evening to say that line...
So the curse didn't work because he spit it all out...
except for the places where it went up his nose?!
Well, great. And that giant oaf just knocked the rest of the cup over...!!
sigh
Oh well.
Guards, just kill my brother now.
stomp
stomp
stomp
stomp

...What?!

It's been fun playing around all these years, Whit.
But I just can't have you alive when the rest of the fam comes home.
I've got a throne to win.
And I was **always** going to win.

I was still injured and exhausted. I didn't have another fight in me.
SWING

I'd had enough of this life, constantly battling and competing...
twist
WHAM!
CRACK!
But in my world, once you let that feeling take hold...
UGH...! That stupid spider woman.
My wounds have reopened...
...you're as good as dead.
HGH—!!
WHAM!

CRASH!!..

I fell into the freezing ocean surrounding our palace and surely would have drowned had I not been spotted by some passing strangers in a boat.

They turned out to be very kind, wise people who changed my life by rescuing me and taking me in to their home...

Who are these mystical beings that helped him...?!

When I regained consciousness, I found myself...

...at a monastery of stoic, male nurses.

The nurses tended to my injuries and provided shelter and food without any mention of compensation.
The tiger curse seems to have mildly spread a certain radius out from his sinuses.
Hmm...Partial curses like that are almost always impossible to dig out.
Best to just leave it be.
So...you're telling me there are **no** female nurses here?
Like... not even one?
Again, no...
While I sat for days as my wounds healed in that barren, painfully quiet room, the events of my past replayed in my head...
...and I continued to sit with just how horrible and toxic my life had been.
I realized I could return home and resume the struggle for power with my siblings, endlessly watching my back at the turn of every corner.
Or I could lose everything and walk away from it all forever with nothing except the clothes I was wearing that night.
One option made me feel much more free.

So I stayed at the monastery.

I didn't know how to do any male-nurse things, but I was strong.

They taught me how to be handy and help out with tasks around the place.

And in turn, the nurses spent a lot of time trying to teach me about things like compassion and self-growth.

Changing your habits is hard.

You need to treat yourself and your thoughts like you'd treat a newborn baby brother. Do you understand?

Got it. So I'd take a [illegible] and [illegible] its [illegible] so it can't ever [illegible] again...

therefore preventing it from usurping my rightful place on the throne years down the road.

—Oops. Sorry about that. Reflex.

What the...?

After a year or so, I felt ready to leave and take the next step forward.

I embarked on a long journey to make amends to as many people as I could who I had hurt.

And through my travels, I eventually pieced together that you had been banished to live somewhere in this small kingdom.
You are the final person I wish to make amends to, Calpernia.

I'm deeply sorry for all the pain and suffering I've caused you.
It's my fault that you live with this curse and that you've been ripped away from your family, your kingdom, and your future.
I would never burden you by asking for any amount of forgiveness.
But I do wish to ask what I can do to make things right for you.

Nothing he's said sounds explicitly like a lie.
But I can't trust what he's saying either...
I felt so much remorse when I believed he was dead. But the longer he talks, the more my blood boils with fury.
Why do I feel this way?

And I apologize for selfishly intruding upon you here. I unfortunately didn't have any means of contacting you first.
I wish there was a way to have sent some type of forewarning or premonition of my intent to come here.

...!!
Premonition...?

Psst...
Prez, what do you think?
H-he seems like he's sorry, and it sounds like he's changed into a pretty decent person...

He is!! He saved me from getting mauled by evil kittens!
Also, it kinda sounds like he could have been camping out near the Pastel Kingdom recently.
Doesn't that fit the description of the potential male club member the spiders found?
And, um...since he's alive and offering to cooperate...
couldn't that maybe reverse your banishment so you can reunite with your fami—
ARE ALL OF YOU **KIDDING** ME RIGHT NOW?!
...!!

You wanna know what I think?! I think you're all being dangerously naive.
And I think you've all forgotten about a certain morbid premonition looming over us...!

SOMETIME BEFORE THE NEW MOON WILL PASS...A MEMBER OF THIS CLUB SHALL DIE IN A FLASH.

I was positive it would happen in a few weeks near the new moon...
which is around when I'd transform into a were-spider again.

But I was wrong.
GRIP
It's clear what the threat is now. And it's time to resolve it once and for all.

drop
drop

step
step
SHAAAAA—

P-Prez...? What are you gonna do...?!
I said we'd politely listen to his explanation about how he survived.
But like all stories...

...it's time for his to come to an end.

So...
Z-zero deaths, Prez...!
Bleeeeeat!
Get out.

If you've been telling the truth, and you really want to make things right with me...
then get out of this forest.
Never come back here, and never tell a soul about this place for as long as you live.
That's all.
...
I understand.
I promise to never reveal any information about this club or its whereabouts.
Thank you for taking the time to hear me out.
And again...

...I'm sorry, Calpernia.

step

step

H-here...
...?

Our jackets are pretty water resistant, so...
You should stay dry. I-if you want...
Thank you...

fwoosh

You should too, though!
Oh. Sure. Thanks...

drip
drop
drip
What is the point of that?

U-um...I know you kicked Whitney out to keep us safe from the premonition.
But he kinda seems like a changed person now...
M-maybe after the new moon passes, we could all discuss the idea of him returning—

I DON'T CARE HOW MUCH HE'S CHANGED!!
My job is to keep everyone in this club safe...
and once someone's been a threat, they can never return—It's as simple as that!!
—!

Darling, do we really have to agree to banish her after this disaster with the Monochrome Kingdom?

She's always been a good daughter...

Well we can't care how "good" she was, dear.

We have to think about the safety of our people.

And now that she's cursed, she'll always be a threat to our kingdom. It's as simple as that!

Uh...so what am I supposed to do? I think she forgot about me...

Am I supposed to leave...?

Now, now. Don't disobey what the scary lady said.

Everyone's supposed to head into the mansion!

Your thick sheep's already inside anyway.

Curtis, do you need some help?

Thank you, Miss Syrah, but I'm almost done bringing things in.

Miss Calpernia wishes to conduct a club-wide roll call for safety measures, though, so please hurry.

dash

All right, you know the drill.
Respond when I call your name so we know who's here.
chk
Aureli—ah, jeez. I gotta update this list...
Abbi!
Here.
Bernadette!
Here!

I saw her this morning...
Hmm, where is she?
Gasp!
Renée?!

I'll think about it at the pond while I feed my swans.

rumble~
I-I know where she is!!
She went to the pond to feed her swans!
What?! That's pretty far from here!
Do you think she's still out there?!
I'll go and find out. Everyone stay put!
dash—

Whoa, I'm going too! We can split up and find her!
Me too!
Abbi, no! It's too dangerous!

They're all gonna run out right now?!!
I'm coming too!!
step

What?!! Gwen, no!!
There's a thunderstorm happening right now!!
catch

But Renée might be stuck out there!!
We can't just leave her all alone—

WILL YOU PLEASE JUST BE SELFISH, GWEN??!
Stop and think of your own safety!!!
And if you can't...well, then I'll go instead!!
...
—Yeah, that's heroic and all...
but you don't even know what Renée looks like, genius.
Th-then hurry! Tell me, what's her thing?! A demon tail? Fly eyes?
...
When we get back, I'm gonna flip you upside down and sweep the floor with you.
And it's a stitched mouth...

Hey! None of you are coming except Saffron, okay?!
We'll be right back with Renée!!
IT'S ABOUT TO HAPPEN...!
N-Nell...?!
pause
What did you just say...?
SOMEONE IN THE CLUB...
WILL...
The premonition?! NO!! WAIT—
...DIE IN A-

The...the pond...
No...it can't be...

Renée...!!
...

This is all my fault...
I focused on all the wrong things...

I'm not protecting anyone—

knock
knock

Hello...?!
open
SHAAAaa—

Um... sorry...
I know you, like, just told me not to ever come back, but...

Renée!
Y-you're **alive!!**
Are you okay?!

...

NO! I'M NOT OKAY!!
I almost died without getting to speak to my best friend again and yell at her for being a big idiot...
unzip~

...and tell her that she should know that when she does stupid, selfish things...
it affects me just as much as it affects her, and that—
plop
plop

Whoa, whoa! You can tell us everything, but just come in and dry off first—

...

You can come in too.
step
step

Chapter 5

A few minutes earlier at the Pastel Palace...

Hey, I gotta skip to the loo. You gonna be okay by yourself, mate?

Didn't take you for such a wuss around thunder...

I...I'm fine...

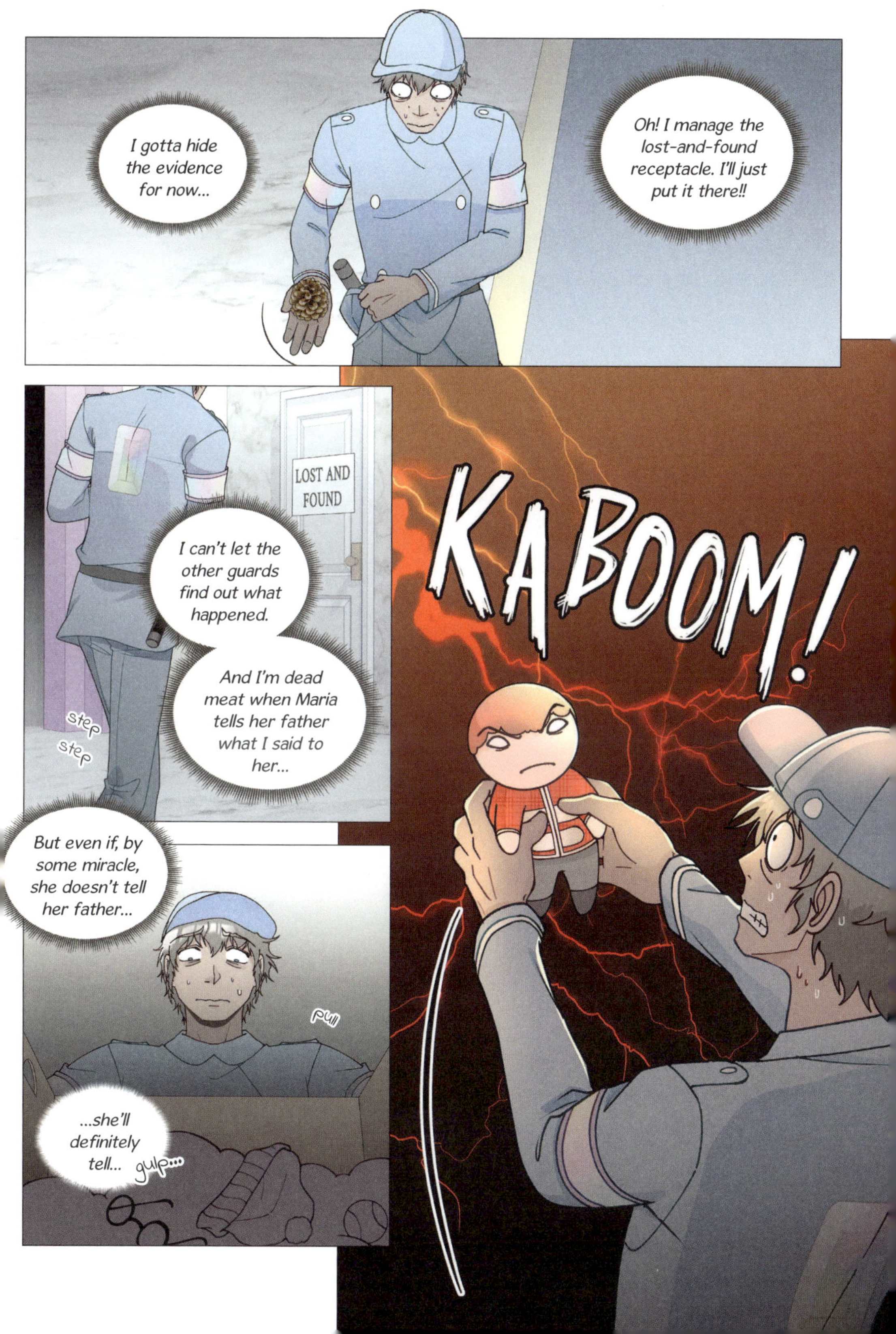

I gotta hide the evidence for now...
Oh! I manage the lost-and-found receptacle. I'll just put it there!!
LOST AND FOUND
I can't let the other guards find out what happened.
And I'm dead meat when Maria tells her father what I said to her...
step
step
But even if, by some miracle, she doesn't tell her father...
pull
...she'll definitely tell...
gulp...
KABOOM!

Hello? Excuse me...?
Hmm, better be preoccupied with something good to ignore us like this...
step
step
turn
...

I don't know!! It's not like I chitchat with them or anything!!

step

step

Right... Great at your job as always, I see.

Guess we'll find out for ourselves.

pant

pant

Oh God. He's on his way to see her now, which means...

the next time he walks down this hall will be for my execution...!

Ready when you are...

But for Frederick to refute a serenade?

That's like refuting the core values of being a Plaid Prince, and I won't stand for it!!

The art of the serenade is about infiltrating stealthily...

taking command of the floor, and capturing everyone by their heart strings—!!

SWING!

...?

Blaine...?

Lance...?

Wh-what's wrong?!

Instead of taking command of the floor, the Plaid Princes sat down on it quietly and listened as the princesses recounted their day.

Back in the forest...

6:30 p.m.

Aww~!

chatter

Here's to a premonition successfully thwarted!!
We did it!! Right, Nell?
Yeah...It's over.
Though it's rare...
It's fine, everyone! Don't forget that Nell's premonitions don't always come true!
Just **mostly.** So let's not panic...
BOOM!
SOMETIME BEFORE THE NEW MOON WILL PASS...
A MEMBER OF THIS CLUB SHALL DIE IN A FLASH.

Sometimes one change to a significant action...

pause

...can open the door for a completely new path.

Get out.

Meanwhile, on the other side of the room...
I-I told you—I didn't mean to push you off that cliff!!
I know what you did!!
You will **not** fool me with your lies or your enticingly fluffy pet llama!

You looked like Gwen, and I was just trying to talk to her, not push her—
slurp~
Bruh, they don't even look remotely alike...
Are you trying to make this worse?

Now, now, I think we've all done and said some things we've regretted.
So why don't we just consider it all water under the bridge, huh?
Instead, let's focus on the thing we all have in common, which is that...

...we all like Gwen.
Isn't that right, Frederick?
Or have you changed your mind after everything you witnessed here today?

Have I changed my mind after everything that happened today...?

...Cursed Princess Club...?!
Wait, then...
They're really kind people who have helped me in a lot of ways.
Honestly, you've got some real nerve thinking that just being chummy with her...
will atone you of everything you've made her go through.
Huh? "Made her go through"?

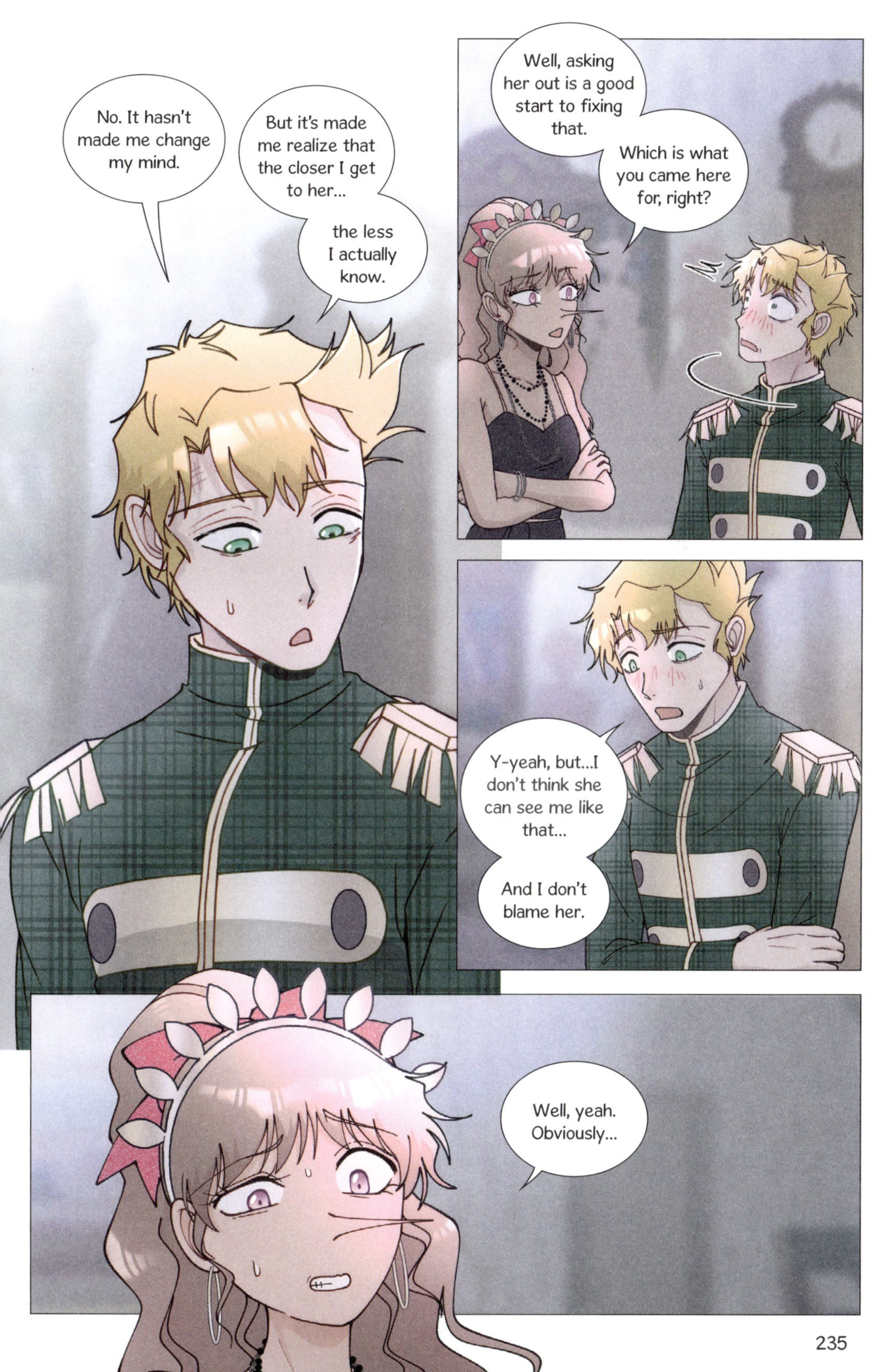
No. It hasn't made me change my mind.
But it's made me realize that the closer I get to her...
the less I actually know.
Well, asking her out is a good start to fixing that.
Which is what you came here for, right?
Y-yeah, but...I don't think she can see me like that...
And I don't blame her.
Well, yeah. Obviously...

Ha, I know. I'm not strong or cool like my brothers.
And I'm done trying to force myself to be like them.
But...what exactly do I offer, then?
I'm not impressive and I can't protect her in any way...
What are you talking about?
You tried to protect Gwen and take her place to look for Renée in the storm.
You also endured the interrogation of some very angry cursed princesses, which is **quite** impressive.

Yeah, but I didn't end up going out in the storm.
And during the interrogation, I almost peed myself like five times...
so I'm not sure what your point is.

My point is that you **care.**
And that's better than any of the other things you listed.

You know...we have some serious issues trusting others...
but self-love is something we actively practice in this club. And maybe you could join us, if you want.
You already know about this place, after all.
Tell ya what. I'm gonna go put in a word for you with the boss lady right now.

step
step
Hmm...maybe Gwen needs a little push too...
Hey, Gwen. We've been chatting with your buddy Fred.
He's pretty silly.
He's pretty cute too, huh?
Oh!! I should check on him!
It's rude of me to leave him alone when he doesn't know anyone here...

—U-uh...

Don't worry about Freddie.

Let Abbi and Monika warm up to him a little more.

Meanwhile, let me spruce up your hair ribbon. It got a little messy from the storm.

O-okay, thanks...

My reflection?
Um, still cracked as of this morning.

I guess I haven't made much progress at all.

Really? I don't think that's true.
I think it's hard for each of us to see our own progress.
But you've been putting in the work.
And I dunno, it may just be about time...

...Time?
For me to love myself and for my reflection to be fixed forever?

Hmm...I don't know about that.
I think loving yourself is something that's never done forever...

But...perhaps your reflection has healed enough to the point where your eyes can start to see some things you may have never noticed before.
Or should I say...

...your eyes will begin to **allow** you to notice some things you never could before.
Allow...?

Do I have feelings for him?
No. I won't ever allow that to happen.

Well, your ponytail has been freshened up, girl.
stand
Now if you'll excuse me, I'm on my way to chat with Prez at the snack table.

What do I eat in the wild? I forage a few leaves and berries, but I mostly hunt meat.
chomp chomp
Organ meat is actually one of the most nutritionally dense foods in the world, though it's an acquired taste...

Butt nugget...?
Hmm...Want us to goad him a little and see if that stoic mask slips?
Yeah, why not?

Sweetbreads aren't actually sweet or bread. It's pancreas.
And head cheese isn't cheese. It is made of parts of the head, though.
step
step

Sooo... Whitney, right? That's a girl's name, you know?

I guess it is.
So is Saffron...

WELCOME TO THE CLUB, BUDDY!!

Hug~

Welcome to the club...

It's up to me, then.

Good thing I can bring the sin out of just about anyone...

Guess I'm just on a roll tonight.

step

step

I was hoping a big, hot man would come to our club.
Thanks for making my wish come true, Whitney.
You're probably busy all the time with the ladies, though. Right?

Um, no. I took a vow of celibacy after I stayed at the monastery.

Oh.
Okay, well...I can toast to that!
What do you like to drink? We got rum, vodka, wine...
Um, mostly rainwater. I just had some outside, though.

I give up, Prez. He's squeaky clean now.
What a waste of all that badness...

...
I **know** it's irrational, but...
I still feel angry. Why?

step
step

Calpernia...?

Hey, Whitney. Enjoying yourself?
In my house...with my friends?

Oh. Yes, I am.

It's been inspiring to see what you've created here...
and how you took your circumstances and turned it into a source of empowerment and security for others.
But...there's also something I wanted to talk about with you.

...

I **told** you. I don't want your apology, so stop begging for forgiveness.
Like you said, I built this club, and I turned into someone strong who inspires others.
I'm doing things I never could have as the Princess of the Polygon Kingdom.

I mean, really, I should be **thanking** you for all of this—

Even if there is some truth to what you said...
...I hope that between all the work you've put in to build this...
you've taken time to grieve for everything that happened to you too.

...

You can feel angry at me. And whatever negative feelings you may have.

I think it's an important thing to express, as long as it's through an action you won't regret later on.

So you want me to express my anger?

In a way I won't regret?

Well, I don't think I'd lose any sleep after giving you one good sock in the face.

How does that sound?

rustle

This party is fun, but I need to remember to take notes on everything.

I've still got my own dinner party to plan...

Perhaps your reflection has been healed enough to the point where your eyes can start to see some things you may have never noticed before...

step
step

Um... Gwen?
...!

Frederick!

H-hey...

Um, here. I got you some juice, if you want.

A-am I interrupting you right now?

Not at all! I'm just trying to figure out how to plan this big dinner party I'm hosting for a school project.

I-it's hard to explain, but it's turning out to be a lot more complicated than I thought...

Oh...! Well, I kinda majored in logistic and administrative support at my academy.
I planned a lot of benefit luncheons...
So, um, if you need any help, I can take a look.
I'm fine!! I don't need you to go easy on me!!
And I specialized in administrative support...!!
Oh, I see. Well then...
thanks for supporting me as I administrate this KICK!
Administrative support...?! That's his game?!
I can't watch this. We almost witnessed several deaths today already...

Really??!! That's so cool!!
Yes, please! I would love your help!
Huh...?
Well, they say it can be attractive when someone's good at something.
Anything, I guess...
Okay, so then you'll want to take your draft budget and build in at least a ten percent contingency in case of emergency...
Meanwhile, you'll want to break down each part of the event into steps, map out any dependencies...
plan out the best sequences of steps needed to complete it, and compile it onto a spreadsheet...
...

Or should I say...
Your eyes will begin to **allow** you to notice some things you never could before...
Allow...?
What things did Syrah mean I'll "allow" myself to notice...?
Do I have feelings for him?
No. I won't ever allow that to happen.
Was that what she was talking about? Because...
...what's the point?
I already know that nothing good can come...
from noticing my feelings...
...for him.

Oh my God. This is the worst mood you could have set.
Gwen looks miserable!!!
You walked over here to ask out the girl you like...
and instead you started helping her do her homework?!

Blaine prepared a fancy serenade for you to dazzle her with...
but **nooo,** you had to be yourself.
YOU'RE THE MOST BORING PERSON YOU KNOW!!

This is so lame...

...!!
I-I'm sorry!! You've done enough!!
What am I doing, selfishly worrying about my own feelings...?!

Wh-what? No, I wasn't talking about—

You've been stuck here in this forest since the afternoon...
and it's all because of me!
You were frightened and injured...

W-well, I mean—
—And I burdened you with all our club's conflicts...
and even made you promise to keep this all a big secret...

A-and now you're even helping me with spreadsheets and contingency budgets...
when you didn't have to do **any** of this—
tug

Gwen, stop!

I'm doing this because I want to!!
Because...

...I like you.

What...?

Th-the reason I came here today...
...um, was to ask you...

That ticket...

But...I...I don't understand...
He doesn't... He can't—

"...some things you may have never noticed before."

"Perhaps your reflection has healed enough...
"...to the point where your eyes can start to see...
Y-you don't have to worry about my feelings, Gwen.
I-it's okay if you don't want to go...

...

No...I'd like to go with you.

Really?

Ahem!
Ladies and gentlemen, a cake has been prepared to celebrate today's numerous victories.
And now that the rain has lifted, I'd like to invite everyone out onto the lawn for dessert and champagne.

AAAAHHH!!!

Gasp
Let's go outside!
It was starting to get stuffy in here anyway...

U-um, I should probably get back to your palace before too long.
My brothers are probably worried about me.
I-I should probably return home soon too...

step step
What about the club president...?
She told me I couldn't leave until she figures out what to do with me for intruding in on the club—

punch
Don't worry, bud. We'll take care of that.
Speaking of Prez, where is she? I don't see her—

Oh. Uh, what's going on here...?!

I'm ready, Calpernia. Hit me as hard as you'd like.
Deal. And I promise we'll call it even after that.
But just to let you know, I feel like hitting really hard...!
Here I come!!!
Where is this lingering feeling of anger coming from...?
The premonition is over. My club is safe. And I didn't murder anyone.

Do I really still hate him so much that I want him dead?
STEP
STEP
STEP
STEP
No. I don't...
Actually...I don't think it's him I'm angry at.
But his death and my guilt...
STEP
...were always the last defenses I could rely on...
STEP
...to hold back the overwhelming feeling that...
STEP
STEP
AAAGGGHHH!!!
I HATE MY CURSE!!!
POW!

SPLAT
...!!!

I HATE TURNING INTO A GIANT SPIDER!
IT FRICKIN' SUCKS!!!

Curtis...!! What's wrong with Prez?!!
My ganache...
I HATE SLEEPING IN A BARN!!

Well, I don't believe anything's wrong.
In fact, I regret that it didn't happen sooner.

After her banishment from the Polygon Kingdom, we came directly to this forest.

Miss Calpernia instantly devoted herself to becoming strong and building the Cursed Princess Club.

I attributed it to a drive and ambition that knew no bounds.

But it took me too long to realize that it was also a way for her to avoid certain emotions she never wanted to face...

Let it all out, Prez!
I think this should be a new club ritual.
I hate thinking about my period so much!!
I could punch a cake or two...

I hate...I hate...
Dang, this cake is tasty.
You guys should really get in on this...

Okay, Prez. We're coming in.
You too, Whitney and Frederick. Don't be shy...
Wow, this **is** good...

Chapter
6

This was not true.

BRAINSTORM SESSION:
HOW TO DESTROY
PRINCE BLAINE'S FIANCÉ

Remember, there are no wrong answers in a brainstorm!

NO BLAINE, NO GAIN

NO BLAINE, NO GAIN

NO BLAINE, NO GAIN

Thank you, Blaine. That's incredibly sweet of you.
But...it's always been a silly childhood dream of mine...
to get to say hello to all the people of our kingdom through music.

...!!
It's okay, though...
Can't you just make me feel better somehow?

...Okay.
I know of something we can do to make you feel a lot better, Maria.
Gasp...!

Wait a minute...
If it's another questionnaire to get to know each other better, I-I'll pass—
No, no, not this time. What I'm proposing is a lot more...um, scandalous.
But only if you would like to, Maria.

YES I WOULD LIKE TO.

But wait, Maria. Are you sure?! There are real risks to this.
And it'll infuriate your father when he finds out what we're doing.
I DON'T CARE!! LET'S DO IT!!!

Okay...! Well, let's still be safe...
We'll wait until he's out of town...I'll come here with the necessary precautions...
Uh-huh! Uh-huh, uh-huh!

—And we'll hold a secret, impromptu concert for you in the Pastel Plaza for everyone in town to attend!!!

—Oh.

...Oh!

Shall we choose your repertoire by the piano?
...Yeah. That sounds wonderful, Blaine.

Sigh
Daddy doesn't think I'm capable of taking over the military when he retires.
...What do you think, Lance?

Hmm...
Well, up until recently, the idea of women fighting didn't sit right with me.
But then you and Suzanna dueled, and that turned out to be awesome.
But still...

...commanding the military?
...!
Maybe I have just been blindly confident.
Just because I like something and I'm pretty decent at it...
doesn't mean I can do it as a career...
I dunno, Lorena. War is really scary stuff.
I can't really blame your dad for telling you that your military studies should just be a hobby...
And what am I saying?! I'm not even that decent at it!
Offensive attacks always make natural sense to me...
but I still can't understand these advanced defensive strategies in my textbooks.
Well, I can at least help with that!
Why don't you bring your textbooks, and I'll go over them with you!
Really? Um, okay. Thanks, Lance.

And so, both couples became deeply absorbed in music and studies for the next hour.
...?
...??

Meanwhile, outside the palace...
rustle
rustle

Frederick and I have been completely silent on our walk back to the palace.
I guess I'm still in disbelief about what happened earlier...

I like you.
Did that really happen...? I would say it has to be a dream, but...
that goes beyond anything I'd ever dare to dream about.
I wonder why Frederick's been so quiet, though...?

Wheeze~
Oh God, we're finally at the top. I can breathe again....!!
How do you travel to and from the forest like this several times a week?!
huff
huff
—Oh! W-well, I don't have to carry a llama...

The only thing I have to do is not let the guards see me come in and out of the forest.
But I think security is still really short-staffed around our palace, so it's not very difficult.
Maybe that's why the guard seemed so stressed out in town earlier today...

You sure you're okay, mate...?
You've been super weird since you came back from town this afternoon.
I'm dead. I'm a dead man standing...
Also, you seem really attached to that doll...

It's been a while since Prince Blaine went upstairs to see Princess Maria.
And by now, he's definitely heard that I confessed to her.
Which means that he'll be coming down any second now to turn my head into crème brûlée...

Please be gentle with my face...

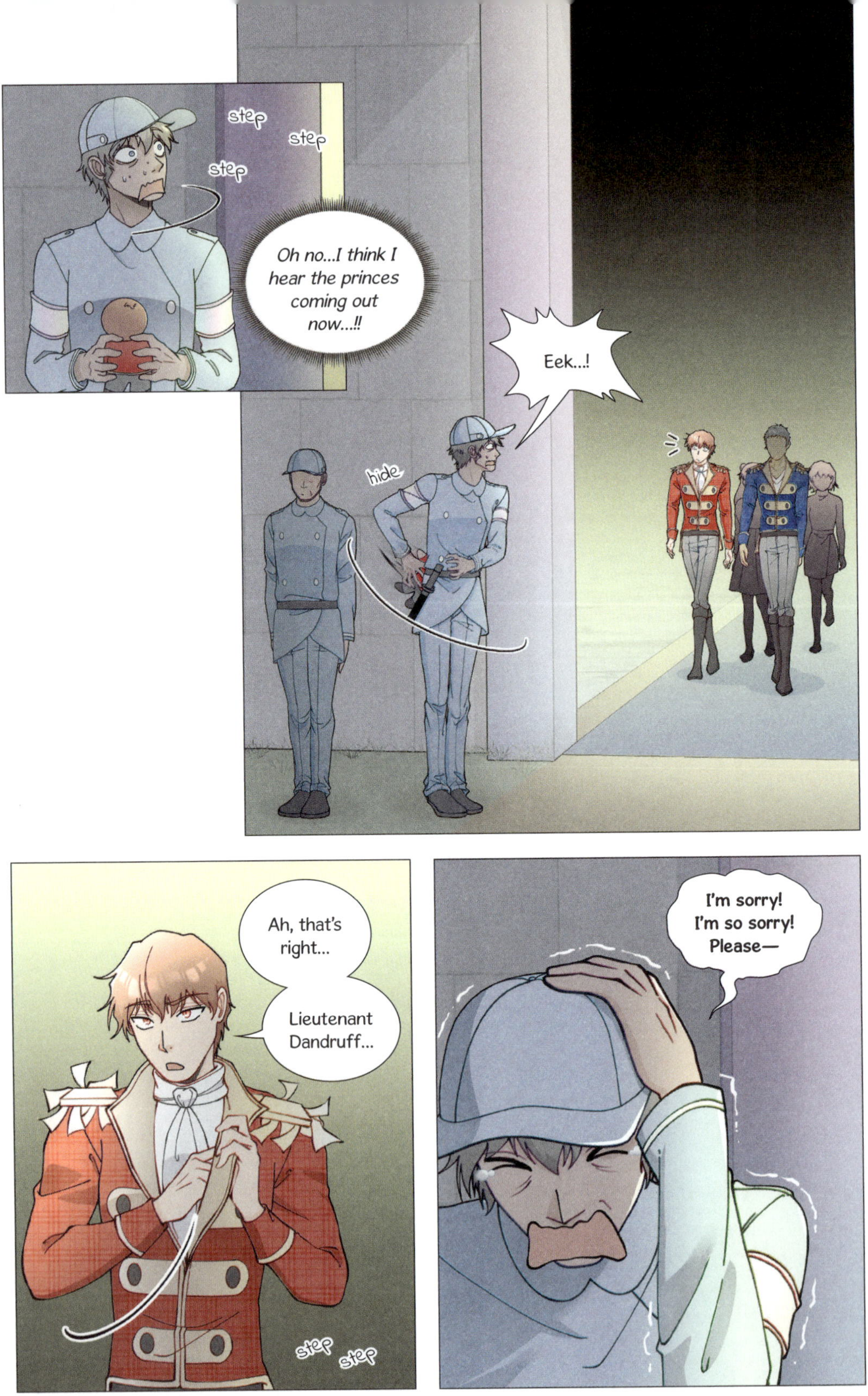

step
step
step
Oh no...I think I hear the princes coming out now...!!
Eek...!
hide

Here.

IT'S OKAY!

It's okay, Lieutenant. I saw the Blaine doll you were trying to hide. But you needn't be ashamed for being a fan.
I understand the stigma that still exists around such things, though, which is why I carry around these supportive flyers for my male audience.
And I shall respect your wish for discretion.
Hey. Let's keep what happened tonight a little secret between us, shall we?

He's showing me compassion and mercy in spite of my feelings for his fiancé...?!
You're a real Prince Charming...

Thank you. Have a good night.
You too...

step step
Do you really have to leave me now, Blaine?
The stars look so romantic now that the storm has passed...
Wait...But the girl he has his arm around...
That's not Maria...

Hey. Let's keep what happened tonight a little secret between us, shall we?
That's what he wants to keep a secret?!!
Real Prince Charming, my butt....
RIP
He's a real two-timing weasel!!!

Looks like our li'l bro succeeded in talking to his fiancé.

He didn't need our help after all.

Hmph...

I think I hear my brothers coming.

Don't worry. I promise I won't tell anyone about the forest or the club.

Thank you...! And I'm sorry again for involving you with everyone like this...

I-it's really fine.
Even if they were a little...**intense** at first, they ended up being pretty nice in their own way...

Y-you don't have to do this. It's only a small scratch...
It's no problem! I always have a first aid kit on me!

I underestimated you. You got game.
giggle
Huh?!

I'm sorry, Frederick. You're a good kid. You didn't deserve all this.
Come back here anytime, and I'll make it up to you somehow!
I-it's really fine!

Hey, Frederick, good to see you again. Wanna meditate?
—Like right now?!!

I'm sorry to you too, Gwen.
Frederick's your friend, and we didn't honor that when you told us.
I think some of us still harbor resentments about being rejected by people in our lives who think of us as monsters...
which is why we're here in this forest.

So when we saw Frederick intrude upon our space, it felt like an attack on us in more ways than one.
But...I think that by continuing to hold on to these feelings...
there's a danger of becoming the very monsters we feared being called.

And besides that...
friends don't get in the way of each other's happiness.
And we want you to be happy, Gwen.

Yeah... they're really nice people in their own way.

Good evening, Gwendolyn!

I'm sorry to bring an end to the evening, but it's about time we took our brother home with us!

Uh, okay! I'm coming!

No, no, adding extra guests eats into your budget and complicates things at every stage of execution.

It's good to keep the guest list as small as possible.

G-got it...

I'll just look forward to hearing all the details later... um, at the gala.

...O-okay.
Right...the ticket.
If I wake up and it's still here, then I'll know...
that this was all real.

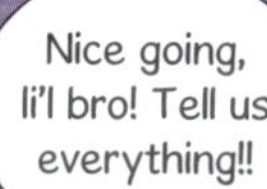
Nice going, li'l bro! Tell us everything!!
There's nothing to tell— Ow, Lance! My skull...!

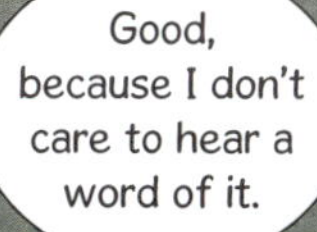
Good, because I don't care to hear a word of it.

open
scurry
Hi, guys...!
Sorry I was gone all day.
Give me attention!!
Pick me up!
Did you get to have your treats? How was your day?
Mine was... um, well...

...stressful...

...scary...

...but also...

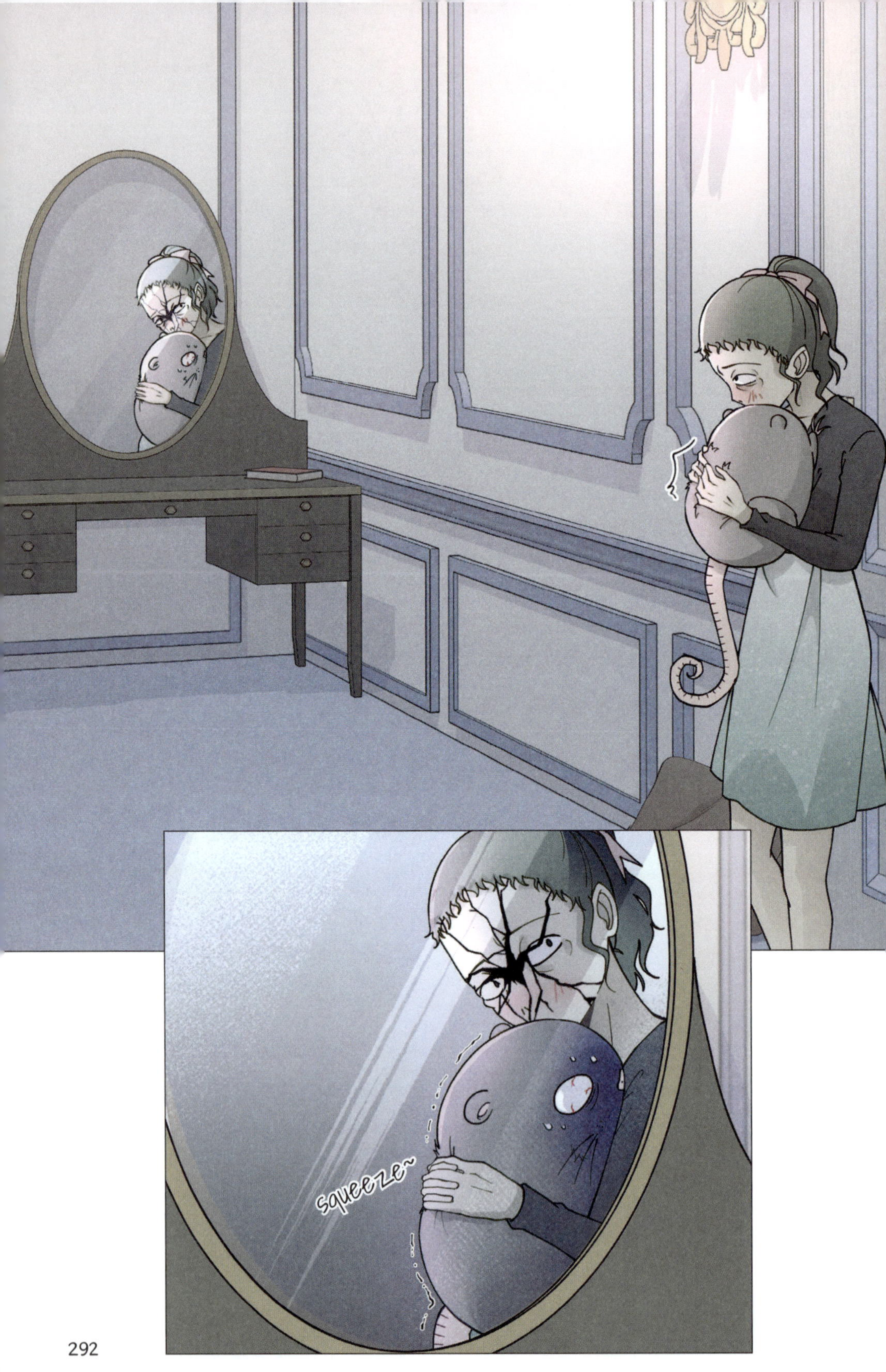
squeeze~

Epilogue

...where he ended up at the local art museum.

King Eugene II of the Denim Kingdom.
drip
drip
At the tender age of 17, he single-handedly fended off a siege by slicing off the legs of 85 men...
which earned him the formidable nickname of "Bootcut Gene."

Wow. I could not be further from this guy...

King Eugene II will be succeeded by his eldest son, Prince "Skinny" Gene III...
who is beloved among the population for his trim figure and handsome face.

Let's see how handsome he looks after I draw a butt on his face...
No!! We promised we weren't doing that anymore!!
That's what almost got us executed!!

I KNOW. I wasn't serious...
I don't wanna have to move again. We just arrived at this crappy kingdom...

...after ol' Ham Hands attracted a fight with those bounty hunters on the lawn of our hideout in the Striped Kingdom.

She did take care of arranging this whole move, though. So it's whatever.
We still need to buy furniture for our new place. We shouldn't be wasting our time here.
Hey, sightseeing is an important part of the moving process that shouldn't be rushed.

step
step
But when we do buy furniture, can we try to find a place where everything isn't covered in denim?

Hmm...
They say one of the best ways to find inspiration is to reproduce the work of great artists.

AAAH!! PINK DEMON!!!
I thought I finally got his terrifying apparitions to stop haunting me at night!
But they've simply transferred over to the mortal realm!!

You SHALL **NOT** haunt me here in my happy place!!

Get back in my nightmares!!!

AAAAH!

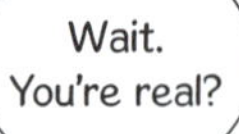

CHAMBRAY CAFÉ

This pie sucks compared to Gwendolyn's.
ALL pie sucks compared to Gwendolyn's.

Hey...but I've been making pies lately...
Oh, I didn't mean yours. Yours are delicious...
Whoa... Check out the dime piece in the booth overthere...

WOWWW~!!

Thanks for treating, Leopold!!
CHOMP

Well, you were looking particularly dejected and pitiful...
like a scoop of strawberry ice cream that fell on the floor.

Well, thanks. This helps.

Don't mention it.

Um...you know what would also help, though...

...is if you could stop trying to sneak vegetables into it.

....!

Dad expects me to take over the kingdom and our troops, I guess.

But I don't know anything about that stuff. Nor do I want to.

I just want to taste food for a living.

Well, I can't blame you.

There isn't anything uglier than war.

Why don't you just tell your father that?

You seem to have no problem causing a confrontation, from what I've witnessed...
Well, sure.
That stuff's fun to do when it's to stand up for my sisters.
But if it's for myself...I dunno. I don't really want to.
Hmm...I didn't know he could have these types of reservations...
Well too bad, Jamie. Self-promotion is part of being an entrepreneur...
which is the job you claim to want so strongly.
And that means you sometimes have to do things you don't want to.
Or is it perhaps that you don't actually believe in your own work?

No...I'm really good at it.

Then you must defend yourself as fiercely as you do your sisters...
and boldly stand up to your father in the way that's most natural to you.

So...with my clothes off?
Please keep your clothes on.
I was thinking more along the lines of showcasing your talents and reputation to him in some creative way.

But...is it really okay for me to shirk all the responsibilities that will be passed on to me...
just so that I can do what I want to do?

Well, you'll have to decide that for yourself.
But it's my personal opinion that nothing can be beautiful if it's done purely out of obligation.

Though I'm in no position to preach.
I recently agreed to an art exhibition solely out of obligation to an associate, and I'm entirely out of inspiration.

That's why I was at the museum, hoping to see if something would fuel my creative spirit.

sigh
But nothing even came from that.
Perhaps I'm not an artistic prodigy but a hack who simply hit his peak at eighteen.

For these hands, which used to never stop creating, have finally ceased to move.
And therefore, it must be time to retire them—

Oh no...
...I believe I have the solution to both our problems.
To be continued in Cursed Princess Club volume 5

Below is a selection of fake profiles submitted by everyone auditioning for the role of Cosmopolitan Princess Conservatory member...

Princess Calpernia
Student

Favorite subject:
Smart Financial Planning for Princesses

Worst subject:
Romantic Literature studies

Favorite beauty tip?:
Your hairpiece can double as a weapon!

Dream career:
School teacher

Princess Thermidora
Student

Favorite subject:
Marine ecology

Worst subject:
Needlepoint embroidery (but I want to get better!)

Notable skills:
Fluent in ~~lobster~~ *a foreign language*

Favorite beauty tip:
Pinch your cheeks for color!

How would you make the world a better place?:
By putting pockets in all dresses

Princess Syrah
Student

Favorite subject:
Puritanical studies

Worst subject:
None, I've been a very good girl

Future ambition:
Definitely not to meet Gwen's hot dad

Quote to live by:
Modesty is the most fun a girl can have

What have you learned about yourself recently?:
That lying even in writing still makes my nose grow.
Can't reach... the paper... anymore

Princess Jolie
Student

Favorite subject:
Black Holes: General Relativity Astrophysics, & Cosmology

Worst subject:
Visual communications

What belongings do you always carry with you?:
First aid kit, mints, lip balm, extra pairs of socks, a spare tennis racket, a tent, a broad sword, a soprano saxophone, a few gallons of water,...

Favorite quote:
"Beauty is in the eye hole of the beholder"

Professor Abbi
Faculty

Courses Taught:
Genius level math

Awards and credentials:
Winner of the Most awesome Teacher award, 40 years in a row

Why did you choose to become a teacher?:
The power

Teaching philosophy:
More recess and no homework for everyone

A message to all of your students:
math sucks and is not useful at all and I hate it

Professor Saffron
Faculty

Courses Taught:
HOW TO DRESS LIKE A DORK 101

Awards and credentials:
LEAST FACIAL HAIR OF ALL TIME

Why did you choose to become a teacher?:
TO BULLY SMALL CHILDREN

A message to all your students:
HEAR YE, HEAR YE, TIS I, PROFESSOR BUTT FACE

my cursed hand stole my pen. can I have a new form?

Volume 4 pencil sketches

An unused idea

Prez's design sheet

LambCat is a small, omnivorous,
and easily frightened creature who has burrowed deep
into the Pacific Northwest to draw comics and make music.
They can be lured out by Bill Evans records and
frosted animal crackers.

Read the original on www.WEBTOON.com

Scrolling not required